Erotic Folktales from Norway

translated and introduced
by Simon Roy Hughes

Erotic Folktales from Norway

Copyright © 2017 Simon Roy Hughes
All rights reserved.

skriket@gmail.com

Version: 1.01

Cover illustration Erik Werenskiold (1855–1938), originally for Peter Christen Asbjørnsen's folktale, "The Companion."
Collophon Typeset in Libertine using LaTeX.

For Inger Anna

Contents

Introduction		**v**
1	The Dung Beetle and the Snail	**1**
2	The Bear	**3**
3	Strange Beasts	**5**
4	The Cock and the Shoe Sole	**7**
5	The Boy with the Mouse and the Flea	**9**
6	Frisk-guss-spass-gass-ber-hu	**13**
7	The Girl Who Served as Soldier and Married the King's Daughter	**17**
8	The Wedding at Velkje	**21**
9	The Tailor and the Bride	**23**
10	Try with Butter First	**25**
11	Adam and Eve	**27**
12	A Lobster	**29**
13	The Woman Who Would Not Fart	**31**
14	To Heaven on My Husband's Pillock	**33**
15	The Wager	**35**
16	The Piglet	**39**
17	The Girl Who Knocked Up the Giant	**41**

18	The Stick in the Barn Wall	45
19	The Girl Who Would Mind Her Maidenhead	47
20	The Foolish Girl	49
21	The Boil on the Finger	51
22	Making Waffles	55
23	The Soothsayer	57
24	The Parson and the Pious Girl	59
25	The Girl Who Knew Not What It Was to Lie with Her	61
26	The Foolish Boy	63
27	The Man Who Expected the Flood	65
28	The Man Who Confessed	67
29	The Quacksalver	69
30	Eggs for Breakfast	71
31	The Humiliated Suitor	73
32	The Parson and the Peasant	75
33	The Tough Sausage	77
34	The Farmhand at the Parson's	79
35	The Charcoal Burner and the Bishop	83
36	Such	85
37	The Spaciously-cunted Kind	89
38	Askeladden	91
39	The Princess's Riddle	93
40	The Pig Boy	97
41	The Sexton and the Boy on the Parson's Wife	101
42	The Boy Who Had So Terrible a Thing	103
43	The Boy Who Herded Hares	105
44	The Boy Who Sold the Bucks	109
45	The King's Sons and the Wishes	111
46	Cabe	115

47	Scruff	**123**
48	The Three Suitors	**127**
49	The Boy Who Served the King for Three Years for Three Shillings	**129**
50	The Boy and the Parson	**133**
51	The Soldier Who Went with a Complaint to the King	**135**
52	The Canny Boy	**139**
53	Hans from Tinn	**143**
54	The Yule Buck and the Girl	**147**
Sources		**149**
About the Translator		**151**

Introduction

IN 1870, WHILE Peter Christen Asbjørnsen was in Granvin in Hardanger, he recorded a folktale told to him by Lars Larsen Røynstrand. Upon review of his manuscript, Asbjørnsen noted his opinion of the tale in the margin: "swinish—useless—obscene." Consequently, the manuscript of "The Girl Who Served as Soldier and Married the King's Daughter" remained in the archives at the university in Kristiania/ Oslo. Similar fates befell the majority of the tales in the present collection; the frank treatment of the sexual aspect of human experience rendered such tales more or less unpublishable.

Some of the tales were distributed, however, albeit privately. Asbjørnsen contributed a number of his erotic tales to *Kryptádia* (1883), where they were presented in German translation. And Reidar Th. Kristiansen printed three tales in *Brudenuggen* (1943). Each of these publications had limited print runs (200 and 13 copies, respectively), and each was privately distributed. *Erotiske folkeeventyr* (1977) was the first general publication of a comprehensive collection of Norwegian erotic folktales, thanks to the archival and editorial work of Oddbjørg Høgset. It is this publication that the present volume is based on.

The designation of the tales as erotic is quite misleading. The erotic concerns an intention to arouse sexual excitement; a cursory perusal of this volume will belie any claim that sexual arousal could be the intention behind the tales. They may be many things, but sexy they are not. Many of them poke fun at the many varieties of human sexuality; others unblinkingly treat the sexual dimension as just one of many facets of human experience. In any case, there is little focus on the sexual act itself. Perhaps a designation as bawdy tales, or as ribald tales would thus be more accurate.

Gershon Legman, a pioneer in the study of this kind of material, would go so far as to erase the distinction between sexual and other folklore:

> The idea that there is a special kind of folklore that is sexual as differentiated from all other kinds, is an optical illusion caused by the operation of a purely literary censorship. No such separation exists in fact. In the field, the sexual material is offered along with all the other material.[1]

The experiences of the Norwegian collectors are consistent with Legman's statement; wherever folklore has been collected in Norway, the erotic varieties have nested themselves amongst the more socially acceptable tales, legends, anecdotes, folksongs, and beliefs. There are at least ten collectors represented in this volume, none of whom has intended to collect illicit material. Their intentions have had little influence on the tales told to them, however. With various degrees of tolerance, they have all recorded what they understood to be unpublishable.

The other collectors represented here echoed Asbjørnsen's acknowledgement of the offensive, unpublishable nature of some of their material. Some struck out certain words in their manuscripts, until they became indecipherable; others spelled out these offensive words in Greek letters, or even Futhark runes; some even protested

---

[1]Legman, p. 240.

in their notes. At the bottom of "The Sexton and the Boy on the Parson's Wife," the collector, G. O. Aaland complained: "I was against writing this, but was pressed to do it." Unless the informant had any compromising material with which he could pressure Aaland, it probably means that the he would not give him any publishable tales until he agreed to record the naughty tale in question. In each case, however offended and appalled they were (or appear to have been), the collectors still archived their manuscripts, implicitly understanding that someone in the future would read them.

We are fortunate that certain people have been interested in bringing these kinds of tales out of the archives, for they are bearers of cultural- and literary significance, as well as being ridiculously entertaining. Their significance rests in their frank treatment of topics that society has deemed unseemly, and proscribed. However, their frankness is a double-edged sword, for on one hand, we have tales that complement what we already know of earlier Norwegian society and culture, whilst on the other hand, some tales appear to be little more than thinly veiled excuses to tell tales of sexual abuse in its various guises.

"The Girl Who Served as Soldier and Married the King's Daughter" is a good example of tales that demonstrate that we still have a lot to learn about our past. As Psyche Ready notes, it is a type of folktale that "does not often appear in published collections, although it has been continuously told for about three thousand years."[2] It is also widespread: "Variants have been collected from locations as distant from one another as Chile, Norway, and Russia."[3] The protagonist is a lesbian who ultimately changes sex, and the tale is ripe for feminist, queer, transgender readings, as it subverts patriarchal precedences of gender rôles, the male–female dichotomy, and family structures.

---

[2] Ready, p. 1.
[3] Ibid., p. 28.

Other tales, too, merit reading from various perspectives. In "The Girl Who Knocked Up the Giant," we are left wondering just how much consent the girl gives prior to the boy "brushing her pussy." Despite her being eager enough after the fact, there is little doubt that she in her turn sexually abuses the giant; psychological perspectives on this tales would be quite interesting. I must note, too, that this tale is one of the most sophisticated, and one of the funniest in the entire collection; there are reasons for reading that transcend any moral or literary value, after all.

Certain tales in the collection add little to our knowledge of the past, though they do confirm what we already know. Tales such as "The Piglet," in which the boy satisfies his lust at the expense of the naïve girl, were considered entertaining, and communicated as such. The same kind of everyday sexism is all too common, even today.

"The Soldier Who Went with a Complaint to the King" is in the same vein. Here, though, what we assume is a rape is extraneous to the plot—take it out, and the tale does not change. In fact, I considered excising this last tale from the collection due to the gratuitousness of the rape episode. After careful consideration, I did not remove it, but instead added a variant (entitled "Hans from Tinn") that motivates the rape by foreshadowing the hero's match with the king's daughter. However, despite the tighter plot, this variant throws up further interpretive problems by equating rape and marriage.

We must remember that all of these tales reflect the culture that brought them forth. In this regard, the rapey tales[4] are as valuable as the tales that we find more appealing and acceptable. Having said this, the majority of them are absurd, hilarious sketches of Norwegian folk-life and -lore in the nineteenth–early twentieth century. They incorporate every aspect of society, not just those considered seemly. I present them, therefore, for what they are:

---

[4] Not a technical term.

insights into the culture, the place, and the time that brought them forth, and a source of—admittedly sophomoric—entertainment.

Bibliography

- Abjørnsen, Peter Christen. *Brudenuggen og andre eventyr*. Oslo. 1943.
- Asbjørnsen, Moe, Nauthella, et al. *Erotiske folkeeventyr*. Oddbjørg Høgset (ed.). Oslo: Universitetsforlaget, 1977.
- *Kryptádia: Recueil de documents pour servir à l'étude des traditions populaires*. Heilbronn & Paris. 12 vols, 1883-1911.
- Legman, G. *The Horn Book: Studies in Erotic Folklore and Bibliography*. New York: University Books Inc., 1964.
- Ready, Psyche. *"She Was Really the Man She Pretended to Be": Change of Sex in Folk Narratives*. MA Thesis. George Mason University, 2016.

— 1 —

The Dung Beetle and the Snail

Collector Tholeiv Hannaas
Informant Torkjedl Asbjørnsen Tonstad
Location Sirdal, Vest Agder
Year 1911

THE DUNG BEETLE AND THE SNAIL were on their way to wet a baby's head. They had washed themselves, and set out early one morning, but didn't arrive. So they had to leave the road and go into a great forest, to find some shelter.

They came to a huge pine tree, and there underneath lay a gentlewoman asleep on her back. The dung beetle crept into the round hole (the lower one), and the snail crept into the other hole (the upper one), and they retired for the night.

As the night drew on, a gentleman arrived and laid the lady. The snail was frightened, and crept as fast as he could, as far in as he could.

When they set out again in the morning, the snail said to the dung beetle:

"You'll never believe how I was set upon last night!"

"How's that?" said the dung beetle.

"Wasn't there a gentleman in with you last night?" said the snail.

"No", said the dung beetle.

"Well, when I was well inside, a spiteful gentleman came in. And he came in bareheaded. I was frightened, so I crept in as far as I could. Imagine it! When he found that he couldn't reach me, he grew so angry that he spat at me."

"Oh, the devil take me! It's not so!" said the dung beetle. "That was no gentleman, but a beggar, for I saw him hang his bag outside my door!"

— 2 —

The Bear

Collector H. H. Nordbø
Informant Nils Smedstad
Location Bø, Telemark
Year 1879/ 80

THERE WAS, UPON A TIME, a man who went to the mountains with a number of fat, gelded rams. Then, when the man had gone some distance, he met a thin bear, which asked how it came to be that his rams were so fat.

"Oh, it's because I gelded them in the spring," the man replied.

It would be good to be so fat, thought the bear, and so he asked the man to geld him.

"No, I daren't do that," the man said. But the bear began to beg him, and the man at last plucked up the courage to geld the bear. The gelding went well, and the man went on his way with his flock of geldings.

In the autumn, when the man was on his way home, he met the bear again. But this time the bear was angry. His scrotum was aching, and he wanted to kill the man.

"Dear me, you mustn't kill me!" said the man.

"Yes. You will lose your life today because you gelded me last spring, and caused me to suffer like this," said the bear.

The man begged pretty-please to be allowed home first, to bid goodbye to his wife before he died.

"Very well then, as long as you hurry back directly," said the bear.

"You may be as certain of it as you are that you sit there," said the man.

When the man arrived home, he told how things had gone between him and the bear. But when his wife heard it, she dressed herself in her husband's work clothes and returned to the bear in her husband's stead.

"Look, I've been gelded now, too," said the woman when she met the bear.

"Let me see how your wound has healed," said the bear.

The woman lifted her smock, and showed her fanny. The bear thought the wound looked terrible, and while he stood wondering at it, a halt hare came hopping by.

"You can stand here blowing on the wound while I go to look for some large leaves to lay on it," said the bear.

The hare did so, but when the bear returned with the leaves, and laid them on the wound between the woman's legs, she let off a fart.

"Oh! Now there's a new hole!" cried the hare.

— 3 —

Strange Beasts

Collector D. M. Aall
Year ca. 1880

THERE WAS ONCE, UPON A TIME, a man who had a troll living under his house, and there was constantly all manner of trouble. The man did not know how he should be rid of the troll; but they met one day, and the man told the troll that he knew of a way, and would drive him out.

"No," said the troll, "but we can wager on the best things for driving. And the one who loses must leave."

So the troll drove with two polar bears. The farmer stripped his wife and the maid, smeared them with tar and down, and placed them on all fours before the sleigh. The troll thought this looked strange.

"But how do you feed them?" said the troll.

The man rode the girl from behind, and she was soon satisfied, but the other horse grew very impatient. The troll wondered about this, but the man explained that it was used to getting its portion first, but that it would not be long before that horse was also fed.

The troll had never before heard or seen the like, and so it had to leave. In any case, the man has not been troubled by the troll since.

— 4 —

The Cock and the Shoe Sole

Collector Peter Christen Asbjørnsen
Informant Ivar Aasen
Year 1883

O NE DAY, THESE TWO spoke together:
"There is none so despised as me", said the shoe sole. "They lay me under people's feet, and they tramp me in the dirt and the mud until I become as soft as a rag. And suddenly I am tramped against steel and sharp stones. Then they smear me around the edges with blackening and pitch. But that's just as bad, for I have to go out both in the frost and the heat. And I never get anything good, except that once in a while, a poor bowlegged fool might pour a dram in me.

"No, I suppose you are treated better. You sit in the warmth of his breeches, and if they take you out, you have a good time. You are petted and stroked by fine hands, and get to play with the ladies."

No, the cock disagreed, and said that the devil would crow if he didn't fare worse rather than better. And it was a miracle that he hadn't worn out a long time ago. Even if he were made of iron and steel, he would never have been able to endure what he had suffered. He had to be awake at all hours, and stand and parade himself, doffing his cap to every strumpet whose belly the farmer wanted him in. And the worst thing was that he drove him up and down in a hole close to the arse. For in there sat one who squeezed with a hoof pincer, and a sucking worm that patted and sucked so that he got so muddle-headed and loose in his stomach that he vomitted everything wet in him. And afterwards, he was so tired and nauseous that he hung like a strand of wet wool.

— 5 —

The Boy with the Mouse and the Flea

Collector G. O. Aaland
Location Lårdal, Telemark
Year 1911

THERE WAS ONCE a princess who was very particular in her choice of suitor. But a farmer's boy thought: I'll catch the princess, I will. So he set off, but he took with him 300 dollars that he had inherited from his mother.

When he had made some distance, he met a man carrying a knapsack.

"What do you have in your knapsack?" said the boy.

"I have something strange in there," said the man.

"What is it?" asked the boy.

"It's a mouse that can do anything you want," answered the man.

"What will you have in exchange for it?" said the boy.

"A hundred," said the man.

"I'll give you that," said the boy, and they traded.

When the boy had gone some distance more, he met a man with a knapsack on his back.

"What do you have in your knapsack?" asked the boy.

"I have something strange in there," the man answered.

"What is it, then?" said the boy.

"A flea that can do anything you want," said the man.

"What will you have in exchange for it?" asked the boy.

"A hundred," answered the man.

"I'll give you that," said the boy, and they traded.

Then the boy came to the king's farm, and asked for lodging, and he was allowed to stay in the domestic quarters. In the evening, the princess came, and ordered one of the domestics to run an errand for her. The boy told the flea to pull his boots off him. The flea jumped to it, but couldn't manage to pull the boots off.

"I'll help you, I will," said the mouse, and grabbed hold of the toe; and the boot came off. The princess stood and laughed at all this.

"You shouldn't laugh," said the boy, "for these will help me win you for my wife."

A very rich and handsome prince had come to the king's farm, and he would present his suit before the princess. She was going to sleep with the prince that night, but when they had retired, the boy instructed the flea to to jump into the prince and princess's bed, and creep into the prince. Then she was to behave herself so badly that the prince shit himself. The flea did so.

In the morning, fourteen doctors were called to look after the prince in his terrible sickness.

The next night, the princess was again to lie with the prince, so the boy instructed the flea to jump into the prince and behave herself even more badly than before. The flea did so, and in the morning, the prince was so ill that it was terrible. And twenty-four doctors were sent for, from far and wide.

The third night, too, the princess should lie with the prince. This time, however, the prince had been more careful. He had made himself some leather trousers, and he had put an ash stopper in his backside. When they had retired, the boy told the flea to get into the prince and behave herself even more badly than she had so far. The flea went, but when she came to the prince, she couldn't get into the leather trousers. So she had to return and tell that she couldn't get in.

"I'll go with you," said the mouse; and they went to the bed. The mouse gnawed a hole in the trousers, but the stopper was still in the way.

"I'm sure I can manage that," said the mouse, "but you must be quick when the stopper comes out," she said. And then she ran up and tickled the prince on his nose, so that he sneezed; and the stopper flew out, and the flea jumped in. And the flea almost killed the prince.

In the morning, the princess said that she could not have the prince; she would rather have the boy in the domestic quarters. So the prince was thrown out in the mud, and the boy won the princess. And they celebrated well and long.

— 6 —

Frisk-guss-spass-gass-ber-hu

Collector Torleiv Hannaas
Informant Olav Eivindsen Austad
Location Byggland, Øvre Agder
Year 1911

THERE WAS, UPON A TIME, a maiden. She did not want a husband unless he had two, for she wanted one left behind if he decided to go off travelling. No one thought it was worth trying for her, for there was none who had two. But then there was a prankster. He arranged himself outside the window, where he knew the maiden stood, and he took out his pole and pissed some on one side of his breeches, then he took it out the other side and pissed.

So the girl tapped on the window for him to come in.

"I think you have two," she said.

Yes, he certainly had, he said.

So they held a wedding, and he had her.

Then he should go off travelling. And he went and wondered; he knew not what he should do, for he had no more than one.

Then he met an old woman. She asked him what he was moping about; what was the matter with him? And so he told how things had turned out for him, that his wife wanted one left behind, but that he had no more than one.

"Oh," she said, "is it nothing more? Look, you can go down to that tussock, there, and take one. There are enough of them. When she wants one more, she must say: 'Frisk-guss-spass-gass-ber-hu! Frisk-guss-spass-gass-ber-hu!' And when she wants it to stop, then she should say: 'Whoa, beastie!'"

Well, he went down to the tussock, and it was full of them; and he came in with it, and hung it on the wall.

Then he got things ready to travel.

When he had gone, and some time had passed, the woman could not hold out any longer; and so she would try this new stick.

She lay in bed. "Frisk-guss-spass-gass-ber-hu! Frisk-guss-spass-gass-ber-hu!" she said. And the pole came off the wall, and set about the woman. But she forgot what she should say to make it stop. So she lay there all night, shouting "Frisk-guss-spass-gass-ber-hu!" until she was so hoarse that she could only just about say "Frisk-guss-spass-gass-ber-hu!"

When the next day came, the maid said to the herdsman, "I don't know what might be stopping madam from rising today."

So she went in to see. There lay the woman, saying "Frisk-guss..." (mostly inaudibly).

"What is it you are saying?" said the girl, "Frisk-guss-spass-gass-ber-hu?" she said.

Then the pole let off the woman and set upon the girl from behind, with her on the floor. She lay shouting: "Frisk-guss-spass-gass-ber-hu! Frisk-guss-spass-gass-ber-hu!"

After the herdsman had slipped the cattle, and neither the girl nor the woman had come, he decided to go in and see what it was that prevented their coming.

There lay the girl in the middle of the floor, shouting: "Frisk-guss-spass-gass-ber-hu!"

"What are you saying?" said the boy, "Frisk-guss-spass-gass-ber-hu?"

Then the pole let off the girl, and came after the boy. Off the boy went, with the pole behind. Then there came a large bull out of a flax field, and the boy wanted to run at him and chase him away, but then he fell on his head.

"Whoa, beastie!" he said.

The pole fell into the flax field.

Thus it is that the women always first cross flax with a cord when they spin; simply because the pole fell into a flax field.

— 7 —

The Girl Who Served as Soldier and Married the King's Daughter

Collector Peter Christen Asbjørnsen
Informant Lars Larsen Røynstad
Location Granvin, Hardanger
Year 1870

O<small>NCE UPON A TIME</small>, a girl desired to serve in the war. They tried to persuade her not to, but it did no good; she wanted to fight for her country and the kingdom, just as any other soldier. Things finally went such that she went; and when she had enlisted, and had been placed on war duty, the king declared war. The girl was brave and beautiful, and worked her way up until she was promoted to captain.

So when the war was over, and the king had won, he gave her a promise that she could choose from the whole army, among the officers, and marry whomsoever she would.

The king's daughter also wanted to marry, and she travelled to the army, to seek out the finest she could find; and she met no one so beautiful as the captain girl. The captain was horrified that she was to be married, for she understood that something was wrong when there came two alike together, but she dared not but obey.

So they celebrated their wedding, both well and good.

Some time passed, and the king's daughter wanted other pleasures, too, but nothing came of it. So the king's daughter was dissatisfied, and said to her father that the captain was too passive, and could not give her any satisfaction. The king asked her to be patient. The captain had but recently been in hard battle, but he would soon recover.

Oh yes, the king's daughter waited, but she longed for her husband to grow livelier in bed. But there was no improvement, he was just as passive as before. Finally she grew very impatient, and asked that he might be given duties elsewhere.

"Well, if it is like that," said the king, "then I know what I can do with him. I have a great tax to collect in a country far away. None who has travelled there under orders has returned, and such will probably be the case with him, too," he said.

So the captain had to travel to the country, however little she wanted to, and collect the tax. She arrived safely, demanded the king's tax, and was paid.

On the road home, she came to a great forest, late at night, and she was afraid that robbers might come and take the tax from her, and kill her. But she saw no sign of shelter anywhere. As she went on in this manner, she saw a light far ahead, and came, by and by, to a small cabin. Then she thought to herself: perhaps I may lodge here tonight.

She understood that they were solitary folk living there. She knocked, but no one opened. She peeped in through the windows, and saw two old folk inside, a man and a wife. She knocked again, and shouted, but nothing helped. The more she banged and shouted, the more they ignored her; they were afraid that it was robbers who would come in to them.

When she understood that she could by no means come in, she pondered how she might best avenge herself on them. Finally, she decided that she would soil the door handle. Thus they would be punished when they eventually did come out.

Then she went and spent the might in the forest.

In the morning, when the two old folk came out, they were so soiled, and stank so badly that they could hardly approach each other. They spoke together about how they would take their revenge on the one who had done this. The old woman said:

"I know nothing worse than that there should grow a big prick on him, so that it hurts him to put it in any cunny."

The man agreed with this, and immediately the captain girl felt it pull, and there was a tumult in her breeches. And when she had a look, there was tackle there, most like a horse's.

She arrived home with the great tax. The king was very glad, but the king's daughter was disappointed, for she thought him of no use to her. But the night came, and they should lie together. Then at last she knew with what kind of fellow she had to do. He nearly burst her asunder. And after that day, there was joy both night and day.

— 8 —

The Wedding at Velkje

Informant Lars Larsen Rønnestad
Location Hardanger
Year 1870

THEY WERE ALWAYS peculiar folk at Velkje, a farm at the top of the knoll, above the church in Graven parish in Hardanger. There was a pair of old folk, one time, and they had an only daughter. She was as big and as huge as the largest of men. Her equal was not to be found among the women of a wide area; but even so, they called her nothing but child—"my child"—and they pampered her and played with her and coddled her, as though she was an infant.

She was to be married, just like the other girls, but it was not easy to find a bridegroom who suited her. Finally they sought out a son-in-law who was just as big and as huge as she was herself.

They were a little simple, these folk from Velkje, and they were therefore barely able to arrange things for the party that came travelling for the wedding. But the bridegroom was there, and he got the kitchen master to invite them in. There was as yet no bench in front of the table in the dining room. Until they could arrange one, the bridegroom sat himself at the head of the table, took out his member, and laid it across the room. Then he invited them to sit and use it as a bench—it seated twelve.

But as they sat, and enjoyed themselves with talk and beer, the bride came in. And her bosom was so large that four lads had to carry it before her, in a baking trough.

When the bridegroom saw them come in like this, his member shot up into the air so that the twelve fell off. Some broke their necks against the eaves in the roof, some fell to their deaths on the the table and benches, but a few survived, though most of them were injured and hurt.

And so there was a funeral instead of a wedding at Velkje.

— 9 —

The Tailor and the Bride

Collector Jørgen Moe
Location Slidre
Year 1845

Once upon a time, there was a tailor who was such good friends with a girl that they wanted each other. But they were not permitted by her parents. The farm was small, that was certain, they said; but she was still a farm girl, and far too good for one who travelled from farm to farm as a tailor, so nothing would come of it.

"Well, try to accept it," said the girl. "Whosoever I am to have, and however things might go, you shall be the bride's friend," she said.

Some time passed, and then she received a suitor. She was to have him, and they drank to their wedding both stiff and strong. The tailor was there, too. But however it was or was not, the bridegroom's companions drank the bridegroom so drunk that he lost nearly all sense and composure.

Meanwhile, the bride's friend lay with the bride in the bed chamber.

Soon the bridegroom missed her, and came weaving out into the bed chamber.

"Are you there?" he said.

"Yes I am," she said. "I lay down for a short rest; I was so tired," she said, throwing herself behind the bed at the same time. The bridegroom threw himself head first into the bed, and groped after the girl's things (so he thought), but he grabbed a fistful of the tailor's...

"But cross and crook! How are you formed, then?" said the bridegroom. "You don't have any tackle that's different from mine. How will this end?" he said.

Well, she was no different from him, said the girl from behind the bed; but she thought it could be fixed. But it would take both time and money to do it.

It would have to cost what it cost, said the bridegroom, if only he might have her in proper condition.

The girl said that she knew a tailor who most likely would take on the work, but then he would have to have her live with him for three months. For the work, he would require sixteen bearskins, sixteen cubits of red cloth, sixteen barrels of salt, and one hundred dollars for his labour; for he had to refurnish her.

They agreed all this with the tailor; and when the three months were up, he came with her and laid her out on the table.

"Now I have fixed her; now she is as good as if she were new," he said. "Come, and I will show you." Then he lifted up her clothes and showed her forth.

"Is there nothing more left of the sixteen bearskins than this small patch?" said the man.

"No, there is not," said the tailor. Then he parted her thighs and showed him the crack.

"Is there nothing more left of the sixteen cubits of red cloth than this?" said the man.

"No, all of it is used up," said the tailor.

Then the man stuck his finger in, and tasted it.

"Well, the salt is there, that's for sure," he said.

— 10 —

Try with Butter First

Collector Knut Nauthella
Location Austevoll, Hordaland

Once, there was a bride who had very tight shoes. Well, there was one evening in the bridal chamber, when the bride and the bridegroom should go to bed, that the bride could not get her shoe off. The bridegroom tried to help, but he could not manage it, either.

"It really is something, how tight it is; I'll have to take a knife to it," said the bridegroom.

"No, no, you mustn't cut it! Try with butter, first!" called the bride's mother who stood without, listening.

— 11 —

Adam and Eve

Collector Knut Nauthella
Location Austevoll, Hordaland

Once when Eve had washed some clothes, she had nothing to hang them on.

He had a pole, said Adam, but it was not supported but for at the one end. He would have to stick it somewhere.

Yes, she had a hole, said Eve.

So Adam poked the end of his pole in there. But as he did so, a wasp came and stung him on the arse. He jumped so that the pole went far into the hole.

"This is good; we should do it more often," said Eve.

— 12 —

A Lobster

Collector Knut Nauthella
Location Austevoll, Hordaland

THERE WAS A MAN who had caught a lobster. He carried it home, and put it in a bucket. Then he put the bucket under the bed, for it was such that the lobster could not get between the edge of bucket and the bottom of the bed.

Another bucket stood under the bed, too, which they used as a chamber pot.

The man had come home late in the night. His wife was already asleep, and thus knew nothing of the lobster. As the night passed, the wife had a call of nature. She pulled the bucket out from under the bed, and sat on it. But she had hardly sat on it before she let out a terrible scream. The lobster had clamped itself fast to the wife's cunny.

The man awoke and ran to her, and would know what the matter was. As he bent down to see how things stood, the lobster lifted its other claw and clamped itself fast to the man's lip. The lobster eventually pulled out a piece from both places. They hurried to take hold of the pieces and put them back again, while they were still warm; and they grew back in place again.

But the man felt that his lip was not as it had been. Therefore, he went to see the doctor.

The doctor pondered his predicament for a while.

"This piece has certainly never belonged here," he said. "It looks as if it belongs to part of your wife, it does."

"Oh, I see," said the man. "Now I understand why, that when my cock rises, my lip begins to quiver."

— 13 —

The Woman Who Would Not Fart

Collector Torleiv Hannaas
Informant Olav Eivindsen Austad
Location Byggland, Øvre Agder
Year 1911

ONCE UPON A TIME, there was a man whose wife was very beautiful, but he dared not go at it with her, for he was afraid that he would knock her up. However, once he got so drunk that he laid her.

Then her belly grew.

So, when the time of her delivery grew close, they were out in the field, the man and their farmboy. He sent the farmboy home, to see how things stood. If she was happy, then he should carry the spade; and if she was sickly, then he should drag the spade behind him.

Well, when the farmboy came home, the wife was very proud; she had given birth to a bonny son. She gave the farmboy some beer and brandy until he was so drunk that it was a spectacle. Then he forgot to carry the spade, but he dragged it. When the husband saw that he dragged the spade, he ran off and beat his tackle against three different objects.

He recovered again, afterwards; but every time he went at it with his wife, she farted terribly, for there was such a large lump on his tackle.

Now, there was an ancient woman and an old man. She asked the wife:

"How is it that you fart so, during the night?"

"Oh," said the wife, "you should see my husband's tackle."

"Well, I bet I wouldn't fart, as old as I am," said the old woman.

"Well, I'll give you a dollar," said the younger woman, "if you can hold it in and not fart."

So they went to do it in the loft; they would try, and see. And the old woman took an apple with her, and stuffed it into her bottom.

Then the old man said, "oh yes; perhaps my wife can now earn herself a dollar, as old as she is." And he stood underneath, this old man, and was so curious, for he thought that his wife might earn herself a dollar.

But when they went at it, the apple shot out of the old woman's bottom, hit the old man in the eye, and knocked it out.

That was some fart!

— 14 —

To Heaven on My Husband's Pillock

Collector Peter Christen Asbjørnsen
Informant Andreas Grøtting (?)
Location Hallingdal

THERE WAS ONCE a couple of folk who had married. But the man had such a short pillock that his old woman wasn't satisfied with it. They discussed this very often, and finally the man had to go to a Finnwoman to get help. There was help there, and so he was given an ointment, as well, that was such that it healed all sores immediately. He was to rub that on if it grew too much and he had to cut some off.

On the road, he met a woman from the mountains, and so he wanted to try it before he came home to his old woman. Well, there was nothing in the way of doing that. So he laid her under twelve inches.

"That was so terribly good," she said. She thought it was a delicious cock, and she thought she could manage a little more. Yes, she should have her fill, he thought. But she had to sit up on top, otherwise it could go right down through her.

When they were finished, she said, "Let it go as far as it'll reach."

"How's it doing now?" asked the man.

"Oh, I'm sitting in the seventh heaven now, old man," said the girl.

"Yes, sit where you're sitting," he said.

After a very long time, he got his cock down again, and it lay limp like eels and sausages in great heaps and piles all around. And there came women-folk from all the villages, and had a go, and went home well satisfied.

At last he came home to his old woman, and she was angry with him, to be sure.

"How have things gone with you, were you made better?" she said.

"Oh, not much," said the man.

However it was or wasn't, they'd have a go, said the old woman. The man added an extra inch, or thereabouts.

"That wasn't so bad," she said, but should he have more, she would like to try it. They would have to change places, then, said the man. They did so, but she hadn't taken any care, so when it got going, she knocked her bottom on the ceiling and screamed:

"Oh! I'm going off to heaven on my husbands pillock!"

— 15 —

The Wager

THERE WAS, UPON A TIME, a man and his servant in the forest, chopping wood. They began to talk about the man's wife at home in the house; and the man said that she would mourn greatly, were he suddenly to die. But the boy thought that she would not mourn so heavily. Women were like that, he said.

Finally they agreed to stage a stunt to decide this, and wagered a hundred dollars each way. The man would pretend to be dead, and should his wife show great grief, then the boy would lose a hundred dollars. However, should she not care too much at all, then the man would lose a hundred dollars to the boy.

So the farmer crept into a long sack that they had with them. Then the boy gathered together the opening, and carried him home, and told the wife that it was the body of her husband he came with. It had come upon him so quickly in the forest, he said, and laid the sack on the floor.

The wife both cried and wept, and was quite moved by this.

"But how did it happen," she asked, when she had ceased weeping.

"Yes, that is a question there is no good answer to," said the boy, and pretended that he would rather not tell her. But she begged and pleaded for so long that he decided to tell her, just as it happened.

It happened like this, he said, that he and the farmer had begun to quarrel about which of them had the largest member. And so they drilled a hole in a tree, and would measure.

"When I stuck mine in, it was so big that it filled the whole hole, but when your husband came with his, he did not even fill half the hole. So we found a wedge, and set it in the hole, so that the hole would be narrow enough. But then it happened that I knocked in the wedge so tight that your husband couldn't get his member out again. He pulled and he pulled, but he remained just as stuck. At last, I knew not what to do but cut off his whole member. But then he bled so badly that your husband died. And now he lies here in this sack," said the boy.

"Oh no, oh no," said the wife, but she did not weep quite as freely as she had done before she heard all this. And soon afterwards, she fell quiet.

"But you," she said, when she had sat a while, "I was just thinking of it," she said, "was it much bigger, yours?" she said.

"It was incomparable," said the boy.

Then they sat in silence for a while; but then the wife said:

"I don't quite know what the matter is tonight; I have had a great shock, and I think it horrible to lie here alone in the cabin when there is a corpse in the house," she said. And she went on in this manner, and paced back and forth, so that the boy understood what she wanted.

"Yes, but there is one thing I must confess, first," he said. "I have such a rotten habit when I sleep, that I am afraid you will not have much pleasure from me in bed," he said.

"What is it, then?" she asked.

"Well, I am terrible to let the wind and the smoke out," he said.

"Really? Don't you think I am used to this from before?" she shouted. "If only you knew of all the sour drinks I have had from him there," she said, and then she ran and kicked the man in his backside, so that it echoed.

But then it was not long before he woke up, the one in the sack.

And he gave his wife a drink more sour than any she had ever had before. The boy, they let him have his hundred dollars. And since that time, the man has never wondered how his wife will mourn him.

― 16 ―

The Piglet

Collector Moltke Moe
Informant Andre Krosshaug
Location Bø, Telemark
Year 1880

THERE WAS A DRUNK MAN who lay sleeping in the roadside ditch. And his thing hung out.

Then there came a young girl who had been into town to buy some meal for her mother. She woke the man and asked:

"What is that, there?"

"Oh, that is a piglet."

"Is it really? Does it eat meal?"

"I suppose it does," said the man.

So she took a handful of meal, and held it out for him.

"No, he is not eating it," she said.

"Lay the meal on your crotch, and you will see that he eats," said the man.

Well, she lifted her dress, and laid the meal on her crotch. And the man hugged her.

"Hau-au, ha-a-au!" said the girl.

"Oh, you don't need to be afraid. It's just the piglet rooting for the meal," said the man.

When the girl came home again, with the meal, she went and got some sweet milk. She poured it into a small trough, and held it between her legs. "Tsa, tsa, tsa, little pig, little pig! Tsa, tsa, tsa!" she said.

"I think you must be mad, my daughter," said her mother. "What are you doing?"

"Oh, I met a drunk man on the road, who had a little piglet, and it ran into me; and now I am trying to get it out again, with the milk," she said.

— 17 —

The Girl Who Knocked Up the Giant

Collector Hans Ross
Location Moland, Telemark
Year 1880

There was a man and a woman who lived alone. They had a daughter and a servant boy, and they had only a cabin with a half-loft. In the loft lay the boy and the girl, each in their own bed, and the man and the wife lay down in the cabin. So one night the girl asked the boy what the commotion was that mother and father made, since the bed creaked so.

"It's nothing more," said the boy, "than that your father is brushing your mother's pussy."

"Couldn't you brush my pussy?" she said.

"I don't have such a brush," he said.

"Can't you buy me such a brush, when you go to the market?" she said.

"Yes, but it is very expensive; it costs a hundred dollars."

"Well, I will soon steal that from father's cupboard," she said.

When he should go to market, she came after him, calling and crying and shouting for him to wait: "Here are the hundred dollars I have stolen from father's cupboard."

So he went to the market with the hundred dollars, and lived well on them. In the evening when he came home again, the girl lay awake in the loft, waiting.

"Did you buy me a brush?" she said.

"Yes, I have bought you a brush, and it is a golden brush," he said.

"Give me it; let me try it," she said.

"You cannot try it; I have to brush you."

"Well, come on, then."

"We dare not yet; your mother and father have not fallen asleep."

But she nagged, and asked again, and so he came to brush her. Her father heard this brushing, and grew so angry that he took a plank of wood, climbed the ladder, and set upon, and began to beat the boy with the plank. The boy fled, and the man followed him, with the plank, and the girl came after them, for she wanted her brush back. The man soon grew weary, and turned back, but the girl continued to go after her brush. So the girl and the boy went after one another, and came over a great bridge across a waterfall. The boy picked up a stone and cast it into the waterfall.

"There is your brush," he said. She began to search in the waterfall for her golden brush, and the boy went on his way.

But then a giant came, so terribly hideous and big.

"What are you searching for?" he said.

"I am looking for my golden brush that I got our boy to buy for me at the market, for he was so angry that he cast it down here."

"I am big, so I can help you wade and search," he said.

So he began to wade and search in the waterfall. But it was very deep and the waterfall splashed on him, so he went ashore and pulled off his wet trousers.

"There! You have found my brush!" said the girl. Grasping hold of him, she pushed him backwards to the ground, then straddled him, and brushed her pussy.

The giant went on his way, full of shame, and the girl went satisfied on hers.

When the giant came home, he told his servant boy that he should go to the doctor and ask which one would be with child, the one who lay underneath, or the one who lay on top. And the boy went to the doctor and asked.

The doctor said that it would be the one who lay underneath. But then the giant was even more perplexed. He pissed into a jar, and sent the boy to the doctor with it, to ask how things stood with the one who had passed the water. But when the boy was on his way, he stumbled and spilt the piss. He stood a while, wondering what he should do now, but then he saw a red cow that stood, pissing in the marsh, and so he held the jar underneath it. Then he went to the doctor, and asked.

"It will be a red bull calf," said the doctor.

The boy returned and told this to the giant, who believed it. He was so perplexed that he decided to go a-wandering until he had delivered the calf. So he took a sizeable knapsack of food, and wandered until there was no more money or food, and his shoes and clothes were worn out.

Then he came to a place where there lay a dead man. He had new boots on, and since the giant had none, he determined to pull the man's off. But his feet were stuck so tightly into the boots that the giant twisted the legs off at the knees. He laid the boots under the flap of his knapsack, and continued.

Late in the evening, he came to a remote moor farm, and he asked if he might stay the night. No, they said, they did not have the room for such a big troll; but he might lie down over in the oven house. He did so, and placed his sack and the boots by the door.

The man and the wife on the farm were up early the next morning, and wanted to slaughter a red calf over by the oven house. But when they had driven the calf over, they had forgotten the water, and so they had to go for that first. The giant woke up in the meantime, and saw the bull calf that staggered across the floor.

"Now I have delivered the bull," he thought, and ran off through the window–he dared not go through the door—and fled from his sack and the boots.

When the man and the wife returned and would slaughter the calf, the wife asked: "What has happened to the man who slept here last night?"

"Oh," said the man, "I think the calf has eaten him up; look, here are his feet, still in his boots."

They dared not slaughter the calf, for they believed there was some kind of enchantment over it; and so they set fire to the oven house, to get rid of it and the calf. When the house began to burn, the calf went into the baking oven and stayed there. And when the house was burned up, it ran unhurt out of the baking oven. Then were the people afraid, and thought that here was something terrible going on. So they fled the farm, and never came back. And I think it is desolate to this day.

— 18 —

The Stick in the Barn Wall

Collector Knut Nauthella
Location Austevoll, Hordaland

THERE WAS A GIRL who was afraid of the boys, so she had a stick in the barn wall that she used.

A boy had noticed this. He knocked the stick out and stuck his member through the hole. And the girl fell pregnant.

When she had the child, they asked her who the father was.

"Isn't it that ugly stick over in the barn wall, then?" asked the girl.

— 19 —

The Girl Who Would Mind Her Maidenhead

Collector Peter Christen Asbjørnsen

O<small>NCE UPON A TIME</small>, there was a girl who was going to a wedding. Little sense had she, and even less they believed she had. So her mother said to her that she should mind her maidenhead, for things could be difficult for a such a young girl at a wedding; the men were so sly when the wedding beer had gone to their heads. Of course she would mind herself, and look after her maidenhead well. And so off she went to the wedding. And there she went, holding her hands before her so that she could neither dance nor drink.

Now, there was a boy at the wedding who knew her. And he liked her, too, for she was a fine girl. He asked her why she went and held her hands before her so that she could neither dance nor drink.

"Well, I will tell you," said the girl. "My mother told me that I should mind my maidenhead, so that the beastly men could not take it from me in the wedding garden."

"Oh, nothing more?" said the boy. "If you like, I can sew the crack shut, so that your maidenhead cannot fall out. And then you can dance and drink and have as much fun as you want—like the other girls," he said.

Of course, she thought this sounded like a good idea. So they went up to a loft, and there he began to sew, both stiff and strong. Finally, he could sew no more.

"No, don't stop; you must sew more," said the girl.

"I can't continue any more," said the boy.

"Why can't you continue, then?" she asked.

"I don't have any more thread," he said.

"What nonsense," she said; "You have two big balls of it," she said.

— 20 —

The Foolish Girl

Once upon a time, there was an old widow who had a daughter who was terribly foolish. The widow fended for herself and her daughter by spinning for others. The girl was naughty, for she wanted to eat up everything, and so her mother would often have to say things such as: "No, we have to save the butter for Yule!" Yes, she supposed they must, said the girl.

Then one day, while her mother took with her all that she had spun, the girl was to stay at home and look after the house. Then in came a poor man, who sat himself on a stump for a chair. His trousers were ripped, and his staff and bag hung down over the stump.

"What is your name?" asked the girl.

"My name is Yule," said the man.

"Oh, is it you who is to have our butter, then?" said the girl.

"Yes, that is certainly possible," said the man.

"But what is this?" asked the girl, touching his staff.

"Oh, that is my sense," said the man.

"And this, then?" asked the girl, touching his bag.

"That is my understanding."

"Oh, could I have some of your sense? Mother says I have so little sense," said the girl.

Yes, of course she could, said the man; and he knocked her off her feet, and gave her some "sense."

When her mother returned home, the girl said: "Yule has been here and has had our butter!"

"Oh God help me!" said the widow. "How little sense you have!"

"No, I don't have little sense, for he pressed his sense into me, and drove it home with his understanding, too," said the girl.

— 21 —

The Boil on the Finger

Collector Peter Christen Asbjørnsen
Location Valdres

ONCE UPON A TIME, there was a girl who had a boil on her finger, and it hurt so much that she thought there had never been such a boil-on-a-finger in the world. She coddled it, she blew on it, she cradled it, and she bound it up like a swaddled infant, but nothing helped. She was suffering as she went. So her mother said to her: "This is just too bad, my daughter; you wander around, suffering, and we have no peace, neither you nor I, neither night nor day. I think it best if you take the horse and buggy, and drive to the doctor for some advice about that finger."

Yes, she thought so too; she took the horse and buggy, and drove to the doctor. When she arrived, she went into the kitchen, and asked to speak with the doctor.

No, this always happened, it did. The doctor had visitors. He was in a card game with the parson and the clerk, and there was no one who dared interrupt him.

Well, it would not help if he was in a card game with the bishop himself, said the girl, for she had a boil on her finger against which all boils-on-fingers would pale in comparison, and until she had some advice for it, there would be no peace. But there was one who was so bold that she went in to him and told him that there was one without who was so ill.

"What is wrong with you?" he said as he came sweeping out with his cards still in his hand, barking like a bound dog.

"Oh, it is this boil on my finger," said the girl. She got no further.

"Oh, go to hell; take your finger, and shove it up your cunt!" shrieked the doctor.

"Yes, thank you very much," said the girl, as she bobbed and curtseyed.

"That was quick advice from a quick man," she said, and then she sat on it, and did what he had said. She whipped the horse, let out the reins, and drove as quickly as the horse could run. Her finger was both sucked and squeezed in the warm room where the boil was, and as she approached home, the boil burst. Then it took some time to heal, until—little by little—it got better.

As the summer drew on, her mother churned some beautiful yellow butter; it was most like an egg yolk. So she said to her daughter: "I think you ought to take a pound of this fine butter to the doctor, for he made your finger well again."

Well, she took the pound of butter to the doctor, and when she arrived with the fresh food (the gifts brought to the country officials were often called fresh food), it was not difficult to get to speak with the doctor. He both thanked her for the butter, and shook her hand.

"But do tell me," he said, "what was wrong with you? I don't quite recall."

"Oh, doesn't the doctor recall?" said the girl. "There was a terrible boil on my finger, which was the worst boil-on-a-finger in the world."

"Indeed, indeed," he said; it was as if he had begun to remember. "But I don't quite recall," he said; "what was the advice I gave you?"

Well, he was soon told.

"Oh, was that you?" said the doctor; she was an able, beautiful girl. "Yes, that was good advice, and thank you very much for the butter," he said; "but neither butter, nor anything else will help me," he continued, "for now I have a boil that is much worse than the one you had, for my boil is on my eleventh finger."

"Oh my dear, poor man, father," she said. "I know what a boil on a finger is like," she said. "But can you not take the same advice that you gave me?" she said.

"Yes, it would be quite straightforward," said the doctor, "but I don't have the same equipment as you," he said.

"You may borrow mine," said the girl.

The doctor thought that was splendid. He borrowed her equipment, and drove it both well and good.

"Ha ha! Now your finger will recover, father," gasped the girl; "I just felt the boil burst."

When she came home to her mother, she told her what had happened, from the beginning to the end; and she was so proud that she had been able to help the doctor with the boil on his eleventh finger, that it was difficult to stay in the same room as her.

"You poor, helpless thing, my daughter," said the woman, as she clasped her hands together; "Now you have lost your honour, too," she said.

"Oh, I don't give a shit about the kind of honour that is so close to the arsehole, mother," said the girl.

— 22 —

Making Waffles

Collector Peter Christen Asbjørnsen
Location Ådalen or Ringerike

THERE WAS, UPON A TIME, a couple of well-to-do folk who had an only daughter. They were so worried for her that she was never allowed to go out among folk. She was not allowed Saturday suitors like the other girls, and she did not know anything. So she did not know how men were formed or made. And she was allowed to learn nothing more than making waffles. But she learned that well.

"You must be careful not to let the revolting manfolk in to you, or you will not be married," said her mother to her. And this she promised, for she would be married.

So then there came a suitor, and after a while, there was a wedding, too.

On their wedding night, the husband wanted to do that which husbands should do, but his wife would by no means have it. He tried all the tricks he had used and knew, but he got nowhere with her. His wife both wept and said that her mother had said that she should never let the revolting men come in to her.

So he complained to his mother-in-law.

"Goodness! Don't you worry about that," said his mother-in-law. "Tell her that you want to make waffles."

Off he went to have another go, but things got worse instead of better.

"Come now, and let us have a change of food; now we shall make waffles," said the bridegroom.

Yes, she wanted to, too.

"I have such a good stick, I do," he said, "and you have such a good little bowl between your legs. We shall make some batter in it."

Oh yes, now there was mixing, and there was baking. But after a long while, he stopped.

"No, no, no, no, no!" she said and nudged him. "Mix, mix, bake, bake, bake, I say!"

"I cannot do it any more," he said.

"Why can you not do it any more?" she said. She was so angry that she both sucked and bit.

"I broke the handle off the waffle iron," he said.

"Ha, ha, ha! I believe it," she said, "for I felt the batter run down my arse."

— 23 —

The Soothsayer

Collector Torleiv Hannaas
Location Bjerkreim, Rogaland
Year 1912

WELL, ONCE UPON A TIME, there was a parson who would hire a farm hand, and he asked what he would have for wages.

Well, he would like to be allowed to fool around with the parson's daughter.

Yes, that would be quite acceptable, for she would never allow it.

Well, the farm hand would wager on that.

"But when I first have fooled around with her, and tell you, then you will not believe it, so how am I then to prove it?"

"Well, we shall place her on a moss-covered log, and let her piss. If she still has her maidenhead, she will be able to piss in a bottle—but otherwise, it will go everywhere."

The farm hand worked out in the field, and when it was time, the girl came out and called for him to come and eat. But one very warm day, when the farm hand saw the girl come out, he lay down on the ground, and pretended to sleep, and he had his tackle out. When the girl called, the boy did not answer, so she had to come further out, and then she saw him. And then she saw his tackle.

"Oh, what do you have there?" she said, and touched it.

"Oh, that is just a soothsayer."

"What does he foretell, then?"

"He foretells that there are some very good cakes underneath that stone over there."

So she ran over, and there lay the cakes.

"But does he foretell anything more?"

"Oh yes. He foretells that there is a wine bottle standing by that rowan tree over there."

Well, she went—and she returned with the wine bottle. All this he had arranged beforehand. So they ate the cakes and drank the wine, and grew merry, and had a good time of it.

"But does he foretell anything more?" she said.

"No, he cannot foretell anything more; he is so hungry that he has to have some food first."

"Oh, what does he eat, then?"

"He is crazy for sugar. Lie down here, and we will spread some sugar on your thighs, and you will see how greedily he eats."

And they did so; and when he had eaten it all on the outside, he went inside.

When he was finished, the girl said, "Oh no, let him eat more; that was so good."

"No, now he is satisfied, and he cannot eat any more this time," said the farm hand.

So the farm hand went to the parson, and said that he had just now been on his daughter. No, the parson would not believe that, so they had to test her. The parson sat her on the mossy log, and she was given a bottle to piss in. But she pissed all over it.

— 24 —

The Parson and the Pious Girl

Collector Rikard Berge
Informant Olav Asbjørnsen
Location Fyresdal, Telemark
Year 1913

THERE WAS ONCE a pious girl who met the parson. And the parson asked the girl, "What is it that can make itself as big as it will?"

"Yes, that I know," said the girl. "It's a cock, it is," she said. "I know it because the servant boy tricked me into holding his. And I held and I held, and had I not let go, then it would have grown so big that it would have filled the whole pantry, and more."

— 25 —

The Girl Who Knew Not What It Was to Lie with Her

Collector Moltke Moe
Informant Andres Lia
Location Bø, Telemark
Year 1878

THERE WAS, UPON A TIME, a man who lived high up in the mountains above Havredalen. He had a daughter who was staying at the pasture one summer.

There came a traveller to her, who would buy some food from her.

Yes, she sold him some, and she received eight shillings for it. But then he wanted to lie with her.

No, the girl did not know what that was, and so he was not allowed. He appeared to be quite satisfied with what he had got.

After a while, her father came up to see how she fared. The girl told him that there had been one there who had bought some food, and for that she had received eight shillings.

"But then he wanted to lie with me," she said. "But what is that, father?"

"Well, I will show you," said the man. He lay at the catch in this.

So he went out and cut himself a pliable switch, and then he told the girl to come. Then he told her he would show her what it was to lie with her. With that, he almost wore the switch out on her.

"So then, that is lying with you," he said.

"Well, if it is like that, then no person shall ever get to lie with me," she said.

Time passed, and she had suitors. And then she was married to one of them.

But then her husband came home to her father one day, and said:

"No, you will have to take your daughter back. I don't want her any more, for I cannot have my way with her. I am in no way allowed to lie with her, and so I don't want her."

"Well, I will advise you on this," said the father. "I have caused it. You should lay a tin plate under her backside, and then you should ask if you might cast a tin plate on her."

Well, he did so, and he was allowed. And when he had had a go, he pulled the plate from under her backside.

A little time later, she nudged him and said:

"You. Can't you cast another tin plate on me?"

After that, he was allowed to cast a tin plate as often as he liked.

— 26 —

The Foolish Boy

Collector Knut Nauthella
Location Austevoll, Telemark

THERE WAS A BOY who should be married, but he knew not what he should do on his wedding night. So he asked his father for advice.

Well, said his father, he should feel downwards over himself until he found something that stood out. Then he should feel downwards over his sweetheart until he found a hole. Then he should stick that which stood out on him into the hole on her.

Well, the boy would try this on his wedding night.

So he felt downwards over himself until he came to his nose. That stood out. Then he felt downwards over his sweetheart until he came to the arse. There was a hole.

So he stuck his nose in her arsehole.

— 27 —

The Man Who Expected the Flood

Collector Rikard Berge
Informant Kjetil Startland
Location Fyresdal, Telemark
Year 1913

It was prophesyed that on a certain day, the great flood should come. And there was a miserly man who would never let poor folk stay for the night.

Then there came a tailor who would stay for the night. But he did not ask to stay the night, not him. He sat down and wrung his hands, and looked very grave.

"Oh God, help us!" he said. "Indeed, indeed!"

"What is it?" said the man.

"Oh, I suppose you know, too," said the tailor, "that the world will end tonight," he said.

"Yes, I daresay it will," said the man.

"Oh yes," said the tailor. "I suppose I have to get going."

"Oh, there is no hurry. I suppose it is just the same that you stay here, now," said the man, "since we don't have long left."

"Indeed, indeed. I suppose it makes no difference. The flood will find both rich and poor," he said.

And so he stayed there, and the man set forth a huge amount of all the food that they had in the house.

Now, the man had made himself an extremely large trough that he hung by a rope beneath the roof. There he lay at night. And he thought that when the flood came, then he would cut the ropes.

During the night, the tailor should lie in the parlour; and there lay the daughter, too. And so he wanted to lie with her, but she was betrothed to a neighbour boy. He came during the night, and wanted to come in to her. But then the tailor covered himself in some of her clothing, and spoke though the window, and said that he was sick.

"Tonight, you must not come to me, for I am so weakly" said "she."

But the boy went home, and got his mother to cook some butter porridge, and he came back with it, and set it forth in a pail. The tailor received it, tipped out the porridge, and shit in the pail. Then he said he was so sick that he could not eat anythng.

Indeed, the boy took it home, but grew so hungry on the way that he would try the porridge. Then he saw that he had been fooled. But he could fool others, too. He took the blade of a plough, heated it until it glowed, and returned for the third time.

"Since you are so ill, then perhaps I may have a kiss from you before you die," he said.

Well, the tailor had nothing against that. It was dark, and he hung out his backside. But it was as if the boy expected this, for he had placed the iron blade beneath him. And the scream was so loud in the house that it woke the man in the trough.

"Here comes the flood!" he said, cut the ropes, and tumbled himself nearly to death.

— 28 —

The Man Who Confessed

Collector Knut Nauthella
Location Austevoll, Hordaland

THERE WAS A MAN who lay on his death bed, and so he would confess for the parson.

"I have cursed a bit, but I have prayed a bit—so we'll call it quits," he said.

"I have stolen a bit, but I have given a bit—so we'll call it quits.

"I have killed a man, but I have sired two—blow me, there I am owed one!"

— 29 —

The Quacksalver

Collector Rikard Berge
Informant Ingeborg Lisle Aasheim
Location Seljord, Telemark
Year 1910

THERE WAS ONCE A QUACKSALVER who was out travelling when he came to a woman who said she was very sick. So the quacksalver would begin his doctoring of her, but first her husband had to go down into the parlour again.

Then he lay together with her, and for his labour he wanted a cheese.

So her husband asked, afterwards, what he had done with her, and she told him. Then the husband grew so tremendously angry that he went after the quacksalver.

"No, not two cheeses from the same farm!" said the quacksalver. And he outran the husband.

— 30 —

Eggs for Breakfast

Collector Knut Nauthella
Location Austevoll, Hordaland

A MAN AND A FARMBOY stood in the barn, threshing. The man worked so that the sweat ran off him, but the boy took it easy; it was always one thing today, and another tomorrow, with him.

"You must work harder," said the man, "or we will never finish."

"You can always play the man," said the farmboy, "since you have eggs for breakfast every day."

Well, if that was all that was lacking, then he could go home and have some eggs, too, said the man.

So the farmboy went.

Now, the man's daughter was at home alone. And when the farmboy came home, he said to her that her father had said that he was allowed to "take her."

No, she did not believe that.

Well, she could just go and ask her father, then. The girl did so.

"Is it true that he is to have some?" she asked.

"Yes, when I have said so, then he is to have some," replied the man.

The farmboy then had the girl lie across the table, and he "took her." Then he went back to the man.

Later, when the man came home, he saw there was something on the table. He wiped it, and then licked it off his finger.

"Is this how careless you are with the egg whites?" he asked the farmboy.

— 31 —

The Humiliated Suitor

Collector Rikard Berge
Informant Tone Kivle
Location Seljord, Telemark
Year 1910

There was a suitor who had with him a suitor's boy. And when they arrived, they cooked fat porridge for them. Now, he was a great eater, the suitor, and he asked the suitor's boy to tread on his foot when he had eaten enough, so that he could stop.

"They have such strange names for the food," said the suitor's boy. "They call a spoon a mound, and a hand they call a fidget, and the food they call pecker," he said. "You must remember that."

Yes, he would.

"It is time to sit at the table, now," they said, "and help yourself."

"Yes, my fidget is such that I can reach the pecker," said the suitor.

As time passed, the suitor suddenly said:

"I have found a hair on your mound," he said.

And the girl answered him:

"There are very many hairs on it; but you will not have one of them."

Then he guzzled the food down, and he was in a hurry, too. And then the suitor's boy trod on his foot. So he stopped eating. But as the night drew on, he grew unreasonably hungry.

"Hey, you were quick to tread on my foot," he said; "I am so hungry."

"No, I did not tread on you; it must have been the cat or the dog," said the suitor's boy.

"Well, I am just as hungry, anyway," he said.

"Then go over and find yourself some porridge, and bring some here to me, too," said the suitor's boy.

But he could not find his way back to the bed. The husband and wife lay at the other end of the cabin, and the suitor's boy got up and untied from their bed the ribbon that the suitor was using to find his way, and tied it to the farmer's bed instead. And she lay naked, the wife, with her backside up, and she lay there, farting.

"Oh no, you don't need to blow on it; it's not too warm," he said, and smeared the porridge on her backside.

But as she woke up, and turned over, her husband thought that she had soiled herself. He grew terribly mean, and made her get up and go out.

But as the suitor found the right bed, he said:

"Hey, my hand is full of porridge. How should I get it off, do you think?"

"Go over to the table, to the beer jug, and rinse yourself there," said the suitor's boy; "they have enough beer here."

So he did so, but got his hand stuck.

"Hey, now I can't get my hand out again," he said; "what do I do now?"

"Go out and smash the jug apart on the white rock outside," said the suitor's boy; "they have enough jugs here."

So he went out, and began to beat the jug against something white. It was the wife, who stood naked outside, wiping herself.

"Oh, I will never do it again!" she said.

— 32 —

The Parson and the Peasant

Collector Moltke Moe
Location Austevoll, Hordaland

ONCE UPON A TIME, there was a parson who, preaching, said that whosoever gave from a willing heart would receive tenfold in return. A peasant sat listening to this, and when the mass was over, he went to the parson and asked if it really was true.

"Goodness," said the parson, "it is!"

"In that case, I want to give you my cow, father," said the peasant. He was not one to have only one cow.

The parson thanked him, and assured him: "You shall have your recompense," he said.

It was such a fine cow, this peasant's cow, and the parson decided that it should be bell cow of the herd. But after a few days, the cow went home, and took the herd with her.

"Well blow me if it isn't true," said the peasant, and so he went out and brought in all the cows.

In the evening, the parson's herdsman came to retrieve the cattle.

"No, the parson himself said that he who gives of little shall receive much in return. He had my cow, and now I have received my recompense," said the peasant.

Well, the parson himself had to come, but things went the same way.

"You shall not have them unless you stand in the pulpit and say that you are a liar," said the peasant.

The parson thought this was a lot to lose, though. And so they agreed that whoever could first greet the other with "Good morning!" the next day, he would keep the cattle.

The peasant went to the parsonage in the evening, and climbed up into a tree that stood outside the maid's window. The parson was a widower.

As the night drew in, the parson came into the maid's chamber.

"Does father come in here?" she said.

"Yes, I do," said the parson.

"Well, you will have to find yourself a place to lie, then," she said.

With that, the parson got into bed with her, and then he began to stroke her pussy, and said, "What do you call this?"

"I call it Jerusalem," said the maid; "but what do you call this?" she said, as she played with his pole.

"Pilate," said the parson.

When it began to grow light in the morning, the parson had to rise, for he wanted to go down to the peasant. As soon as he came out into the courtyard, the peasant climbed down from the tree.

"Good morning, father!" he said.

"How long have you been there?" said the parson.

"Since Pilate entered Jerusalem," replied the peasant.

And he was allowed to keep the cows.

— 33 —

The Tough Sausage

Collector Knut Nauthella
Location Austevoll, Hordaland

THERE WAS A MAN who had a daughter. But he was so afraid that the boys would take her that he had her with him in his bed at night. She lay against the wall, and he lay outside her.

But then this girl had a sweetheart. And when she expected him, then she asked permission to go out on an urgent errand.

Yes, she was allowed.

So she met the boy, and he had her up against the barn wall, and "took" her like that.

But there hung a scythe up on the wall, and because of all the shaking, it fell down, the scythe. And it fell between the boy and the girl, and sliced off the boy's member.

Then the fun was over. The boy went on his way, and the girl went back in to her father. But as she stepped over her father, as she climbed into bed, the boy's member fell out.

"What is that, there?" asked the father.

"Oh, it's a stub of a sausage that I took," said the girl.

The father tried a bit. "Blow me if that isn't a tough sausage," he said.

— 34 —

The Farmhand at the Parson's

Collector Peter Christen Asbjørnsen
Informant Andreas Grøtting
Location Hallingdal
Year 1865

ONCE UPON A TIME, there was a parson who was so miserly that he would not buy a bed for his farmhand; he had to lie in a bed with the daughter. But therefore, he had to have one who was gelded.

So he went out and should try to find one to go into service, who would be of advantage to him, rather than do some damage. He met many, and all of them would go into service with the parson, so they said yes. But when he then asked if they had anything to come with, you should understand that they did no say no to that. But when they had such, and were not gelded, there would come nothing of it. Then the parson would not have them in his household, he said.

Then there was one who was more sly and cunning. And he put out a rumour that he was supposed to have said that he had nothing. And then he turned aside, turned his clothing inside out, and went back another way. And just like that, he met the parson.

The parson did not recognise him, and asked the boy again if he wanted to go into service with him, and if he was gelded.

"Yes, of course," said the boy.

"It is very good that I came to you," said the parson.

He wanted him as his farmhand, and he had to go home with him immediately.

As they were on their way home, the parson asked the boy what his name was. "Oh, I am ashamed of my name," he said.

"A name shames no one," said the parson.

"No, so I have heard," said the boy, "and since father really wants to know, can I tell him. But handsome a name it is not; my name is Cock."

"No, that is truly not a handsome name," said the parson. But they need not use it from day to day, he said. They could call him "farm boy."

When the boy came into the kitchen, the first thing the parson's wife asked him was his name.

"Oh, I am simply ashamed of my name," said the boy.

"A name shames no one, is what I have always said. We must know what to call you, when we call you in to dinner."

"Yes, well handsome a name it is not; but since the parson's wife really wants to know, then my name is My Cunny," said the boy.

"Well, you may be right; a handsome name it is not. But we can call you 'farm boy' from day to day," said the wife.

Just like that, the parson's daughter came in to the kitchen, and wanted to see the new farm hand. And it was hardly strange that she should be curious, since she would be having him as bed mate.

Well, the boy said to her, as he had the others, that he was ashamed of his name, but eventually it came from him that his name was Father Crawl on Mother.

They lay now in an upstairs room, these two—the farm hand and the parson's daughter. And no sooner had they had gone to bed, than that the bed began to creak. The parson lay downstairs and heard this.

"What is going on, my daughter?" he asked.

"Oh, it is just Father Crawl on Mother," said the parson's daughter; and no matter what he asked, and no matter what he said, she had no other answer.

"What nonsense!" said the parson. "Do go up, mother, and see what is going on," he said.

"It is My Cunny, who is on our daughter," she said, when she came up into the loft.

"Yes, Father Crawl on Mother is scratching my cunny so nicely," said the parson's daughter.

"It is quite normal for it to scratch at your age," said the parson.

"Oh no, father, it is My Cunny who is on our daughter," said the parson's wife.

"I believe I shall be able to stop you," said the boy. He took the parson's wife, heaved her on to the bed, and did the same to her that he had been doing with the daughter.

"What is all the noise?" said the parson.

"Oh, My Cunny scratches so nicely," said the parson's wife.

"Aren't you ashamed, at your age, speaking like that in front of the child?" said the parson.

But it got worse, rather than better, the tumultuous noise, and so the parson had to put on his dressing gown and trousers. But when he came up the stairs, the boy jumped out the window, and was gone.

On Sunday, they went to mass, and were in church, listening to the sermon, both the parson's wife and the daughter. Just like that, the daughter grew very happy and glad, for she had seen the boy behind the altar.

"Father, Father Crawl on Mother, behind the altar!" she cried.

"Hush, hush, my child! You must not speak in that way in this place," he said, and hushed her.

But she pointed, and when he saw the boy, he grew so wroth that he banged his fist on the pulpit, and shouted:

"Every man, get Cock out!"

He meant that they should drag the boy from the church.

The congregation glared sternly at the parson, and wondered what this might mean; but he banged the pulpit again, and screamed it even louder.

So yes, they unbuttoned their trousers and did what they thought he had meant they should do. And then the boy began to laugh.

"Now My Cunny is laughing!" said the parson's wife.

"Yes, if she's not laughing now, then she'll never laugh," said the boy.

— 35 —

The Charcoal Burner and the Bishop

Collector Moltke Moe
Informant Thomas Aarmoti
Location Åmotsdal, Bø, Telemark

ONCE UPON A TIME, there was a charcoal burner who felled and burned charcoal. But he did not like it, and so he decided that he would rather be a parson. Well, they let him be one, too. But he was not much good as a parson, don't you know. And the congregation was dissatisfied, and wrote a complaint about him. So the bishop came to hear him, to see if what they had written was true; and so the charcoal burner should preach a sermon.

The charcoal burner lived modestly. And when the bishop came, he was to lie in the bed, whilst the charcoal burner should lie on the bench. Now, the charcoal burner had an unreasonably fine wife, and as the bishop lay, he spoke with her. Then he went over to the charcoal burner and pinched his nose, and then took a smoldering shingle and put it in his beard so that it singed it away. All this was to see that he slept. Yes, he lay still.

Then the bishop lay on the wife's bosom and asked, "What do you call these?"

"I call them Samuel's Bells, father."

Then further down.

"I call that the Grey Babylon."

So now the bishop was with her, and took care of her that night.

The next day, Sunday, was the day the charcoal burner was to preach his sermon. And the bishop sat there to listen to him.

"There came a man to me yesterday," said the parson in the pulpit. "And he pinched my nose, and set fire to my beard. And then he rang Samuel's Bells, and afterwards he went into the Grey Babylon."

"That is enough, my man! You are good enough to preach," said the bishop. And thus the charcoal burner kept his position.

— 36 —

Such

Collector Moltke Moe
Informant Gonne Dalen
Location Bø, Telemark
Year 1878

O NCE UPON A TIME there was a man who was on a journey, and his wife was expecting. He could not come home before she had delivered the child, and so he arranged to wet the baby's head, and did both the brewing and the baking.

While he was away, the parson came to the wife and said, "Oh God help you! Your husband has forgotten to make a nose for the child."

"Really?" said the wife. "How will things go, then?" she said.

"Oh, if you will give me everything that has been made for wetting the baby's head, then I am sure I will be able to think of something," he said.

Yes, he could have it all, and so the parson made a nose for the child.

When the man came home, he asked how things had gone.

"Oh yes," said his wife, "but you had forgotten to make a nose for the child, you had," she said.

"Indeed," said the man, "I had forgotten that."

"Yes, but the parson came along, and he got everything that had been prepared so that he would make a nose for the child," she said.

"Well, since he has done it…" said the man.

Soon the parson went on a journey, so the man went to the parsonage while the parson was away. He went into the kitchen.

"Good day," he said.

"Good day," said the kitchen maid. "Who on earth are you?" she said.

"Oh, I am a cunny-gilder."

"Really?" she said. "How much do you want, to gild it?" she asked.

"A hundred," he said.

Well, he should have it.

"Right, lie down wide open on the floor," he said. And then he placed eighteen eggs between her legs, and the nineteenth he stuck into the hole.

"So, what are you called?" she said.

"Oh, I am Such; but now you must lie still, and not move until I return," he said. And with that, he went in to the parson's wife's parlour.

"Good day," he said.

"Good day," said the parson's wife. "Who on earth are you?"

"Oh, I am a cunny-gilder," said the man.

"Oh, how happy it will make father, when it is gilded," she said. "How much will you have for it?"

"Two hundred," said the man.

He knew the parson had a new-born foal, and so he went down to the stable, cut off its head, and stuck it in the hole.

"What are you called?" asked the parson's wife.

"I am Such, I am; but now you must lie still, and not move until I return," said the man. And with that, he went home and arranged a leather sack, which he filled with liquid manure. Then he took it out at around the time he thought the parson would return. Then the parson and his driver boy came.

"What is that you are carrying?" said the parson.

"Oh, this is courage, it is," said the man. "I would not be too long without it."

"So what is it, then?"

"Oh, I tip it over my head when I am sorrowful," said the man, "and then I am comforted again."

"So that is courage," said the parson. "Will you sell it?" he said.

"Well, I don't know about that. I only have a little of it. But if you give me three hundred, you shall have it," said the man.

Yes, that was fine.

When the parson came home, the gate was locked, and those inside dared not move until Such came. So the parson's boy had to climb over the gate, and he went into the kitchen.

"Have you seen Such?" said the kitchen maid.

"No, I have never seen such; and God help me, I'll never see it again!" said the boy.

Then he went into the parlour.

"Have you seen Such?" asked the parson's wife.

"No, I have never seen such; and God help me, I'll never see it again," said the boy; and then he went out to the parson.

"How do things stand?" asked the parson.

"Well, this is how things stand," said the boy. "The kitchen maid is lying wide open on the kitchen floor, and has laid eighteen eggs, and the nineteenth is in the hole. And your wife is lying on the floor in the parlour, and is giving birth to a foal; I could see its head."

"Oh God help and comfort me," said the parson; "now I am sorrowful." And with that, he lifted the sack above his head so that the liquid manure ran down over him. And now the parson goes beshitten every day, unless he has washed himself.

— 37 —

The Spaciously-cunted Kind

Collector Knut Nauthella
Location Austevoll, Hordaland

THERE WAS A BOY who visited his sweetheart every Saturday evening. She lay in the bedchamber, whilst the man and his wife lay in the adjoining parlour.

Well, he had a bottle of brandy with him, and he laid it in the girl's bed, while he undressed. Then the girl sneaked a draught from the bottle. And when the boy took the bottle again, he felt that it was lighter.

"Aha! There have been folk here before me!" he said.

"No, it's not that; it's just that we are of the spaciously-cunted kind," shouted the girl's mother from the parlour.

— 38 —

Askeladden

There was a princess who was always so haughty, and he who would win her should make her laugh. And this she was allowed by her father. Many tried, but none of them was successful.

So you understand that Askeladden had also to have a go.

He walked and reflected on how he should do it, and then he came to a forest where there lived a wife who had a little magpie.

"What is it that you are reflecting on?" asked the wife.

"Oh, I do so want the princess. If only I could make her laugh," said Askeladden.

"There must be a way," said the wife. "I have a golden magpie that is so pretty that everyone would like to have a feather from it. And then you should say, 'Hold fast, like the old wife taught me!'"

And he was given a ribbon to lead it by. There the magpie went must also all those who held on to it follow.

Then there came a fine girl walking. She cared not for the boy, but she wanted the magpie.

"You have a nice magpie, there," she said.

"Yes, isn't it nice?" said the boy. "Do you want a feather?"

"Yes," said the girl, and she went over to the magpie.

"Hold fast, like the old wife taught me!" said the boy, and thus she was stuck fast.

Askeladden led the magpie onwards, and the girl came along behind.

Just like that, there came a knight, riding. He thought it was strange, but of course, he wanted to help the girl, so he dismounted and went over to her.

"Hold fast, like the old wife taught me!" said the boy, and thus he was also stuck fast. One hand held on to the girl, and the other hand held on to the horse; and he was all but naked, for the girl was so unreasonably gorgeous that he had already taken off his trousers. He had, of course, no idea that he would be stuck fast like this.

When they neared the castle, they met a kitchen girl who was on her way out to get a sausage. When she saw the knight nearly naked, she thought he had stolen the sausage, and she went to take it from between his legs, and so she was stuck fast to his member, for the boy had said, "Hold fast, like the old wife taught me!"

Then another kitchen girl came out with a wooden spoon, and when she saw the kitchen girl with the sausage, she was so angry that she wanted to smack her on the bottom.

"Hold fast, like the old wife taught me!" said the boy, and so she was stuck, too. She began scream and carry on, and then she wanted to get off, for she had a call of nature.

"Hold fast, like the old wife taught me!" said the boy, and so the bucket was stuck to the kitchen girl's backside.

Now the boy had got what he wanted, and he went up to the castle.

They all came out, and they laughed until it was unpleasant. The princess also came out, and was so astounded that she forgot everything, clapped her hands together, and laughed.

"Yes, now you're mine," said the boy; "now you have no excuse."

So she understood that there must be enchantment involved, and gave in. And then I could no longer keep up.

― 39 ―

The Princess's Riddle

O NCE UPON A TIME, there was a king who had a daughter who had three gilded cunny hairs. This king's daughter had many suitors, but the king would not give her away to anyone before they had guessed what she had. Out in the forest close by the king's farm lived an old wife, and she had a son. The king had arranged a meeting for the suitors, so that the one who was best at guessing what the king's daughter was created with should have her.

The old wife out in the forest had three little pigs. One day she said to her son that he should take one of the pigs to the king's farm, and try to sell it, for she thought that they might need it at the meeting of the suitors. The boy went to the king's farm with the pig. He met the princess outside.

"Will you buy a pig from me, princess?" asked the boy.

"What do you want for it?" said the princess.

"Will you lift your skirts so far up that I can see your calves?"

"Yes, you may have that," said the princess, and then she lifted her skirts, and the boy was satisfied.

When the boy came home with no money, his mother was very angry. But the boy said that he would do better another time.

The next day, the boy should go to the king's farm to sell the second pig. When he came to the king's farm, he met the princess outside.

"Will you buy a pig today?" asked the boy.

"What do you want for it?" asked the princess.

"Oh, if you will lift your skirts above your knees, then you shall have it," said the boy.

The king's daughter did so, and the boy was satisfied.

When he came home and told his mother how things had gone that day, she was angrier than the day before. But the boy promised that he would do better another time.

On the third day, the boy should take out the pig she had left. When he came to the king's farm, he met the princess outside.

"Will you buy a pig today?" asked the boy.

"What do you want for it?" asked the princess.

"Oh, if you will lift your skirts up to your belly, then you can have this one, too," said the boy.

"That is high up," said the princess; "but will you come with me out back?"

"Yes, I will," said the boy, following her.

The king's daughter lifted her skirts, and the boy saw the three hairs.

The day came, and the suitors met at the king's farm; and the king took them into the great hall. The boy from the forest also met up, and he asked the king if he might come in, to listen.

"No, you may not," said the king.

"I can stand in the hearth, if I may."

"Well, so be it, then," said the king, and the boy came in.

Then the suitors began to guess, and they guessed and they guessed.

And then a minister guessed that the king's daughter had three hidden things.

"She has three gilded cunny hairs," said the boy in the hearth; he dared not hold his tongue any longer, for he felt they would guess it.

Then the king grew exceedingly angry, and asked the boy how he could know that.

"Well, I know it as surely as I know that the king has today eaten three pigs," replied the boy.

"Yes," said the king, "then my daughter shall lie between the boy and the minister, and the one she has turned towards in the morning shall have her."

When the night drew on, the boy said: "I need to get up and shit. But how shall I do it when the door is locked?"

"Oh, you can do it in the hearth," said the princess; "you are a pig anyway."

"Well, it has to come out, what went in, even though you be a princess," said the boy.

So he got up and went over to the hearth. There had he a bag of all kinds of fragrant things that he anointed himself with. Then he lay down again beside the princess.

A little while afterwards, the minister said: "I also have a call of nature; I think I have to get up," he said.

"Yes, do so; you can do it in the hearth, for we can blame the boy," said the princess.

So the minister got up and relieved himself in the hearth, and then he went back to bed.

But then the boy said: "Since you will give me the blame, then I will up and eat what I have done," said the boy. And then he got up, went over to the hearth, and anointed himself with all these fragrant ointments, and then he went back to bed.

But then the minister lay there, thinking, and then he said to the princess: "Now that the boy has eaten his, I think I must do the same, for we cannot blame him now." And then he got up and began to eat, and then he lay down again beside the princess. But then he stank like a whole latrine, and so they slept. But the princess had to turn towards the boy, and she lay and licked around his mouth in her sleep.

And when the king crept in, in the morning, and saw that she lay turned towards the boy, he said: "Now you shall have my daughter and half my land and kingdom."

So they held a wedding for eight days; and I was there for six, but then I had to come here and tell of this courtship.

— 40 —

The Pig Boy

Collector Moltke Moe
Informant Aslaug Dalen
Location Bø, Telemark
Year 1878

ONCE UPON A TIME, there was a woman who had some pigs to sell, and so her son should take them out. So he took one pig, and went with it to the king's farm.

Then the queen came out.

"What do you want for it?" she asked.

"Oh, I don't want much for it," said the boy. "If I may see the king's daughter to her knees, you shall have it," he said.

"What use would you have of that?" asked the queen, reluctantly.

Oh, it would be of no use to him, he said; but that did not matter. If he got it, she would have the pig.

Well, he got it, then.

Then the woman was so mad at him that it was a spectacle, for he had not taken payment for the pig.

So on the next day, he took the second pig, and went to the king's farm with it. Things went the same way as they had on the first day. The queen came out and asked him what he would have for the pig. Well, said the boy, if he could see the king's daughter up to her thighs, then she would have the pig. The queen said, now as before, that she did not understand what use that would be for him, but he got his will in the end, and the queen got the pig.

His mother was no happier when he came home this time. But on the third day, the boy took with him the third pig, and went to the king's farm with it. Things went the same way as they had the first two times; but now he wanted to see the king's daughter to her navel as payment.

When he came home for the third time without payment for the pig, the woman was so mad that she chased him away. She had no more pigs.

So he went to the coutyard of the king's farm, and said: "I know something," he said. "I know something, me."

"Quiet! If you will be quiet, you shall have as much money as you want," said the queen, and gave him a sack of money.

Then the boy went home to his mother and said: "Here is payment for the first pig, mother," said the boy.

The same thing happened on the second and the third days.

Then there should be a great feast at the king's farm. The king's daughter should be married, and the one who could tell what kind of cunny hairs she had should have her. But no one could.

"Well, here is no one left," said the king, "except this boy, and I don't suppose he knows anything. But he may try, too."

"Well," said the boy, "the king's daughter has one cunny hair of silver, one of gold, and one of bronze."

"How can you know that?" said the king.

"Oh, I do know it," said the boy.

But then he could not have her anyway. Both he and a knight should lie together with the king's daughter that night. And the one she had turned towards in the morning should have her.

So in the evening, the king locked them in. As the night drew on, the boy said: "Ow! I need to shit so much that I don't know what to do. I think I shall have to shit on the table."

So he got up and cut a honey cake into a big pile on the table.

A little while later, the knight also had a call of nature. And it was not feigned, either.

"Well, I don't know what else you can do except that you do it on the other end of the table. Otherwise, there will be a huge pile," said the boy.

So that is what the knight did.

Then they lay a while more. Then the boy began to quake, and then he said: "Oh, I had a terrible dream. I dreamt that the king came in and would kill us because we have shit on his table. I don't know what to do except that we each eat up our pile."

And with that, he got up and ate up his honey cake. Then the knight went and put in him that which he had laid on the table. But then he smelled so bad that the king's daughter had to turn towards the pig boy.

So in the morning, the king came in: "But what are you doing?" he said. "Have you not turned towards the knight, then?"

"No, I could by no means endure that," she said; "he just smells of shit."

So there was a great feast for four fortnights, and for two shorter days, and for one very short day. And if they have not finished, then they are still at it.

— 41 —

The Sexton and the Boy on the Parson's Wife

Collector G. O. Aarland
Location Lårdal, Telemark

O**NCE UPON A TIME**, there was an old parson who married a young miss. But as the old parson could not satisfy her, she used the sexton and a servant boy. But when these two discovered that they both had the wife, they agreed that whichever of them could take her most in the presence of the parson, he should have her to himself.

The sexton should try his luck first. No sooner said than done. It was late one autumn evening that the sexton came to the parsonage, and went in to the parson. The parson asked if it was the sexton who was out walking so late.

"Yes," answered the sexton, "but as I went past the window, I thought I saw the parson laying his wife on the sofa. But it could not have been."

"No, certainly not, no," said the parson, "but now I want to go out and look," he said.

But when the parson went out, the sexton took the wife, and laid her on the sofa. When the parson came in again, he said that he thought he saw the sexton laying the wife on the sofa.

"No, certainly not no," replied the sexton.

"Those windows are going out during the day tomorrow, since they distort so horribly," said the parson.

So the sexton went to the servants' cabin, and told the servant boy Hans how well he had done.

Then it was Hans's turn.

One day, Hans was carrying threshed grain to the barn. And the parson wanted to go for a walk with his wife. Then, just like that, Hans came, carrying a sack of grain.

"He is a strong one, Hans," said the wife.

"Yes, he is a powerful fellow," replied the parson.

"Hah! This is nothing," said Hans. "I could just as well carry the parson, and his wife, too," he said.

"That I would like to see," said the parson.

"Then come," said Hans.

So Hans took an empty sack, and bent over to put it on. And then he put the parson lying with his belly against the sack, and then he put the parson's wife with her back against the parson's back, and then he took the wife on the parson's back. And thus it was that Hans won.

— 42 —

The Boy Who Had So Terrible a Thing

Collector Moltke Moe
Informant Andres Lia
Location Bø, Telemark
Year 1878

ONCE UPON A TIME, there were three brothers who were very stubborn, and they wanted their inheritance. But their father would not give it to them before it was time. But they nagged and they nagged until finally their father was weary of their nagging, and gave them their inheritance.

The elder two took their money and went out trading; but Oskefisen bought pats of butter with his inheritance, and lay down and buttered his pole and cultivated it until it grew so big and huge and fat that it was a coarse thing. He had it three times around his waist.

Then his brothers came home.

"Do you lie here?" they said to Oskefisen. "Look at the money we have earned. You could have made just as much, had you come with us, you utter pig."

But Oskefisen just lay there and buttered his thing.

"But over there in a guesthouse, there was a woman with such a large cunny that it was terrible," they said. "There are many who have wagered with her for great sums of money that they could satisfy her in bed. But she won over them all. That would be something for you!"

Yes Oskefisen lay a while, listening to this, and then he roused himself and went off to the guesthouse. And he sat down to drink and play cards with the guesthouse woman. And they eventually wagered six-hundred on whether he could satisfy her in bed.

Well, he got himself ready, and unwound his thing, and then they went at it in the bed in the cabin. And they carried on there until they had moved across the floor and out the door and down the stairs and out in the hall and out in the courtyard and down a steep hill that lay by the house there. And so stubborn were they, that neither would give in, so they continued. But there was a marsh at the bottom of the hill, and Oskefisen got her into a boggy hole, and kept on going.

But she would not give in.

So Oskefisen shouted up to the house:

"You must come with my coat; I am going to work into the winter, here!" For he had laid aside his coat up at the house.

But when the woman heard this, she was afraid, and said:

"Oh no! I suppose I had better give in, then. I have lost!"

And that is how Oskefisen won the six-hundred dollars.

— 43 —

The Boy Who Herded Hares

Collector Gunnhild Kivle
Informant Tone O. Kivle
Location Seljord, Telemark
Year 1911/ 12

ONCE UPON A TIME, there was a boy who served at the king's, and he herded hares. There was one time he should travel home. When he was on the road, he met an old woman who asked if she might have some food from him.

"Yes. I have but little food, but what I have you shall have," said the boy.

So the woman had the food, and ate it all up. Then the woman said:

"Well, since you were so kind that you gave me your food, you shall have a pipe from me. When you blow it in the evening, all the hares will come to you."

Well, the boy thanked her, and travelled to the king's farm, and he herded hares. During the day, he sat on a mound, and in the evening, he blew the pipe. Then all the hares came home in the evening. And they were astounded. But they soon knew that the boy had a pipe that he blew. And the king's maid went to the boy, and would have the pipe from him.

"Yes, but I must lie with you," said the boy.

So he was allowed.

"And now, I must have it," said the girl.

"Yes, now you may lie with me, as I lay with you."

She did so.

"So now we are quits," said the boy. And she went on her way, full of shame.

Then came the king's daughter. Things went the same way with her: he lay with her, and she with him. Then he said that they were quits, and then she left.

Then the queen herself came. And things went exactly the same way now: he lay with her, and she with him. Then he said: "Now we are quits." She was terribly full of shame, and left.

Then the boy told this to the king: "I should have your daughter!"

"Yes, if you can sing this vessel full, then you shall have her"

Well, this was not the agreement, said the boy, but he began to sing thus:

> And the king sent his maid to me,
> And I lay with her,
> And she lay with me,
> But still I kept my pipe.
>
> And the king sent his daughter to me,
> And I lay with her,
> And she lay with me,
> But still I kept my pipe.
>
> And the king sent his queen to me,
> And I lay ...

"Halt! Halt! Now it is running over," said the king.

And the boy won the daughter of the king, and they feasted, and that greatly.

I too was at the feast. And I should help with the baking. I was so terribly stubborn, you know. Then I was supposed to go up on the cabin with a sack of peas. As I came up the stairs, the bottom fell out of the sack, and all the peas ran all over the floor. Then I should have some bread and butter. Then they called that I should fetch a pail of water. Then I laid my food on the stove, and when I came in again, it had nearly all burned up. The butter ran, and the bread burned, and I had not a crumb. So I wanted a little more, but I didn't get any. Then they grew so mean to me that they loaded me into their gun. Then they shot me over to the lingonberry cart. And if you won't believe it, then you don't have to.

— 44 —

The Boy Who Sold the Bucks

Collector Knut Nauthella
Location Austevoll, Hordaland

THERE WAS A BOY who should go into town and sell a buck. But it was far to the town, and so he spent a night in some place where there was only a girl at home.

The girl asked him if he wouldn't rather sell the buck to her.

Yes, if he were allowed to "take her," then she could have the buck.

No, he could not do that.

Then they argued a while about it. In the end, they agreed that he would be allowed to see her as far up as the top of her socks, and then the buck would be hers.

The next day, the boy returned home. His father asked if he had sold the buck.

Yes, he had, but he had not got the money yet; he would have it tomorrow.

The next day, he said he would be off to collect the money. But then he arranged to take another buck with him. This one he would sell, he thought.

In the evening, he came in to the same girl. She asked now, too, if he would sell the buck to her.

No, sell it he would not, but if he were allowed to "take her," then she could have the buck.

They argued a while about this, and finally agreed that if the boy could see her pussy, then she would have the buck.

The next day, the boy returned home. Then his father asked if he had the money for the buck.

No, he had not got it; but tomorrow, he would go and get it.

The next day, he went to get the money, but now too, he arranged to take another buck with him. This one he would sell, he thought.

But now, too, he came no further than to the same girl.

This time his father had stolen along after him, for he had noticed that the bucks were gone. When the boy went in to the girl, his father climbed on to the roof.

Now, too, the girl asked if he would sell her the buck.

No, he would not, but if he could "take her," then she could have the buck.

No, he could not, but they spoke at length about it, and finally he would be allowed to stick the tip of his member in her pussy.

"Oh, just press it all the way in!" said the girl, when she felt how it was.

No, the boy would not.

Yes, if he would do it, he could have all three bucks back again.

Still the boy pretended that he would not.

"Just do it! Just do it!" shouted his father. He lay, watching down the chimney.

— 45 —

The King's Sons and the Wishes

Collector H. H. Nordbø
Informant Nils Smedstad
Location Bø, Telemark
Year 1879/ 80

ONCE UPON A TIME, there was a king who had three sons. The elder sons lived in luxury, but the youngest, Oskefisen, had to do the heaviest work: look after the horses, and bring water for them. Then once, when he was fetching water, he got a fish in the bucket.

"Oh, dear heart, release me, and I will grant you what you will," said the fish.

Well, Oskefisen did so; and he wished that he could make his thing as big or as small as he wanted. Then he told this to his brothers.

"Oh, you great fool! Could you not have found something better to wish for?" they said.

Then the eldest went out for some water, caught the fish, and wished for money. The middle brother did likewise.

Then the two elder brothers went out, to court a king's daughter who was so used to it. Oskefisen wanted to go, too, and was not allowed. But he followed along anyway.

Then he came to a guesthouse, and asked if he might buy some food.

"Yes," said the girl, but he had to wait until the fine gentlemen who were inside had been served theirs. So he had some food. Then he made his pole so long that he could circle her waist with it, and asked how much the food would cost.

"Tut! Don't even mention it," she said. "But if you will sweep me off my feet and have your way with me, then you shall have it for nothing, and you shall have this tablecloth, besides. It is such that when you unfold it, it fills up with the costliest of dishes."

So Oskefisen "paid" for the food, and thanked her for the tablecloth.

Things went the same way at the next guesthouse. There he got a cockerel-formed beer jug that was such that it was never empty, for his services. And also at the third guesthouse, the girl wanted the same payment for the food. She gave him a pair of scissors, too, that were such that when one snipped with them, out came the finest clothing.

Then they arrived at the king's daughter's. His brothers laughed at him, and advised against his trying for her hand: "She will only put you on the island of rejects."

And she did, too.

Out there, he fed everyone who had already arrived, from his table cloth. So when they came with food for them on the next day, no one wanted it. The servants went over to the king's farm and told this.

"It must be the one we sent over last," said the princess.

"No, no, not him. It must be one of the others," said his brothers.

But they brought him, and asked him. Yes, he showed them the tablecloth. The king's daughter would buy the tablecloth. But no, it was not for sale, but if he could lie with her atop the bearskin, then she could have it.

No, he could not, but he could be released and never go back to the island.

No, that was no good; Oskefisen would not concede. If she was afraid, then she could have her guards in the room.

So that is how it happened; and Oskefisen lay cooing all night. And the next day, he was put back on the island.

Things went the same way with the beer cockerel. But then he wanted to lie with her beneath the bearskin. And when she wanted to buy the scissors, the price was that he should lie between her legs.

No, *that* would certainly not happen.

Well, it was not dangerous. He had nothing to do any damage with. He showed her his thing, and the doctors said that he could do nothing.

So yes, then he would be allowed.

Just as he lay, he made it big and pressed it in. But he lay cooing so quietly again. And it tickled, don't you know.

"Oh, draw a stroke," she said.

And he did.

"Oh, draw a stroke," she said again.

No, he would not.

"Oh, draw a stroke," she said a third time; but he would not.

"Well, now you have stood there for two night," she said to her guards. "You must be by weary now; it is best you go and get some sleep. You know he has nothing to do any damage with, anyway."

So they left, and were happy to go.

"Oh, draw a stroke," she said when they were alone.

Yes, now Oskefisen was willing.

"And one more."

No, he would not.

"Oh, one more stroke," she begged.

But no, he would not. It made no difference how much she begged.

"Well, it is all the same," she said. "If you will have your way with me, then you shall have me and the kingdom and everything I have."

Yes, now he did what she asked of him, and that is how Oskefisen won the king's daughter.

— 46 —

Cabe

Collector O. T. Olsen
Informant Nils J. Olsen Bjeldaanes
Location Rana, Nordland
Year 1870

In the east, there once lived a very wise man whose name was Cabe. He had a habit of fooling or making a fool of anyone he would. His reputation for this soon spread across the whole country, and eventually it reached the king's ears. He had no faith in such gossip, but said: "Cabe must fool whom he will, but he will never fool me!"

And so he set himself the task of trying Cabe, and bringing his great reputation to ruin. Therefore he chose some men whom he could trust, and took them with him to visit the famous Cabe.

Meanwhile, Cabe had also heard of this plan of the king's. And quick-thinking as he was, he made a decision to fool the king. Cabe owned an iron cauldron, large and reasonably heavy. This he made glowing hot, and took it out and stood in the road where he believed the king would have to pass. He put the cauldron on a stump, and filled it with water, which was quick to boil. And a little while afterwards, the king came.

The king, who did not know that this was Cabe, stopped and spoke with him. All the while, Cabe threw one piece of meat after the other into the cauldron, which continued to boil until it eventually boiled over.

The king marvelled aloud over such a spectacle, the like of which he had never seen before. And he asked Cabe how it could be so.

"Oh," said Cabe, "such things happen at my command."

"And without wood," said the king.

"You understand," replied Cabe, "that with wood, any old cauldron will boil."

"Will you sell your cauldron?" said the king; "I will pay well for it."

"Well, I would hate to lose such a property," said Cabe, "but for the sake of the one who asks, I can hardly say no."

"What do you want for your cauldron, then?" asked the king.

"A hundred dollars," replied Cabe.

"Here is your money, and my thanks. Now I must go home and try my new cauldron," said the king, "and let Cabe go unvisited. Good day, my good man."

He arrived home and commanded that they should fetch his fattest calf and slaughter it; "for," he said, "a new cauldron and good meat go well together!"

He cut the meat into the cauldron himself, and waited and waited for it to boil. But in vain; the cauldron did not begin to boil. Now he realised that he had been fooled, and he hurried off to find the trickster.

When he returned to the same place, he met the man. He approached the king with such elegant politeness that the king's wrath subsided. The man appeared much grieved that he had forgotten to tell the king that it was not only the cauldron, but also the stump that summoned the power for the boiling.

"I would not sell it," he said, "for many hundred dollars, in these wood-free areas, where one must pay dearly for each and every stick of fuel. But to assuage my shame, I will sell it for half its value, or for two hundred dollars."

The king agreed the terms, paid the money, and returned home, happy with the valuable stump. Now he filled the cauldron again with meat and water, put it on the stump, and anticipated that it would soon begin to boil. But in vain. The king now understood plainly that he had been fooled. Angry, he started off again to visit the man, and avenge himself for the prank he had played on him.

When he had come a distance on the way, he heard a man who cursed terribly, caring not about the king's presence. The king turned aside and admonished the man; but he, on account of the king's admonishment, grew all the more angry. He pulled out a long knife from his belt and stabbed first his mother and then his sister, and these fell as dead to the earth, blood streaming freely from them both.

When they had lain a while, he went to them and began to scratch across them both with his knife, and then they began to show signs of life. They were soon both completely quick, and approached the man with great humility and begged forgiveness for their impertinence.

The king wondered greatly at what he had seen, and asked the man how such things could happen.

"Oh," said the man, "I usually discipline my folk in such a manner when they are disobedient. Then they are so humble and pliant that I soon have manifold compensations for my trouble."

The king still did not know that this man was Cabe, who had agreed with his folk to tie bladders of blood beneath their clothes, and who had fooled the king with both the cauldron and the stump. The king longed every day to meet Cabe, and understood that this man's knife could be useful for something eventually. So, in anticipation of meeting Cabe, the king asked the man if he would sell this wondrous knife.

"Only reluctantly will I part with it," said Cabe; "but since it is the king who wishes to own it, I will not say no."

"How much do you want then for this seldom treasure?" asked the king.

"Well, its value," said Cabe, "cannot be estimated; it is, of course, priceless. But for the king's sake, I will sell it for three hundred dollars."

"Well, here you have the money!" said the king, and he took the knife and went home happy, to try its power on his disobedient household. First they should be punished, and then, soon afterwards, even Cabe might learn some respect.

As soon as he came home, the queen began to scold him in the most dreadful manner, but as she could not defend herself against his scorn, one of his two sons came forward to help his mother, and defend her from the king's rage. But, even more bitter on account of his son's behaviour, the king pulled out his newly purchased knife, and pushed it first into his son, and then into the queen. Both soon fell dead to the ground. The king's servants fled in terror, but by his command, they had to return.

After a little while, the king began to scratch along and across the dead, to recall them to life. But all was in vain; they were and remained dead.

The king now understood that it must have been Cabe who had played him all these pranks, and in his grief and wrath, he swore that Cabe would hang. He went now again to visit Cabe, and this time, he found him, too.

Cabe was taken to the king's farm and held there until the following day, so that as many people as possible should have time to gather together and watch his sticky end.

In the evening, he asked the king if he would not grant him the grace to go to visit his old mother a final time before he ended his days. The king granted his wish, and allowed him to go once more home to his mother. But he was accompanied by a numerous and strong company under the strictest orders not to let Cabe out of their sight.

So he came home to his mother, to bid her farewell. But on the return journey, he said to his guards, as they approached an old mill, where Cabe knew there was always an old man watching the mill: "I have two things to ask, and I am certain you will grant me my wishes. The first is that you allow me to go by myself into the mill, for there to hold my devotion and prepare for my death. And the second is that you thereafter never disturb me with unnecessary questions or conversations. In the mill I shall wear a blindfold so that nothing may divert my thoughts from the confession I shall make in the coming hour."

With the permission of his guards, Cabe now went into the mill and closed the door behind him. Thereafter he went to the old miller, assumed a serious demeanour, and said:

"To heaven and to paradise I will not go."

"Oh, then you are a fool!"

"Yes. Come and take my place," said Cabe.

"With all my heart," replied the old man.

Then Cabe said: "We must swap clothes, and then you must not speak a single word when you come out of the mill."

"And why so?" asked the old man.

"Well, it is only on these conditions you can come to paradise," replied Cabe.

"Well then, the mill shall cease its chatter before I cease my silence," said the man.

They swapped clothes, and Cabe bound a kerchief before his eyes and let him go out.

Cabe's guards took the old miller now, and brought him with them, and when dawn broke at the king's farm, they quickly strung him up. And thus he ended his days without having spoken or made a sound.

Now the king held a great feast for all his friends, and rejoiced with them because Cabe had finally been rewarded justly for his misdeeds.

In the meantime, Cabe stole the hanged man and buried him.

"Look, look!" said the king, when he heard of this. "Even a Cabe has his friends!"

He would rather not have Cabe's friends as his enemies, and he decided, therefore, to do good for Cabe's kinfolk. So he sent Cabe's old mother a large sum of money. His sister he would have in service, but she would not go to him immediately. She needed some time, she said, to arrange her clothes. When this was done, she would soon come.

In the meantime, Cabe dressed in his sister's clothes and went to the king. The presumed girl was welcomed kindly, and told to go into service as a maid for the princesses. She excelled quickly, with her efficiency and order, and that to the degree that the king recommended that his daughters follow her example and advice in everything. Therefore, during the days, they were always with their new tutor, and at night they slept in the same chamber.

One evening, when they had gone to bed, one of the princesses said: "I don't know what to do, for I often dream of men."

"Well," said Cabe, "if any of us dreams of men tonight, then we will move two and two into the same bed. Then we shall see if we cannot be delivered from such dreams."

No sooner had they fallen asleep than the eldest princess awoke and shouted: "Ack! I have just dreamed of men!"

Cabe went therefore to her and slept with her that night. The next night the youngest dreamed of men, and Cabe had to sacrifice that night on her. And thus it continued, night after night, for some time.

Then it happened that the king's son fell in mortal love with the new mistress of the house, and he decided that he would have her by any means. He proposed and received a yes. But he had to promise not to make any attempt on her until after the wedding. The king's son hurried therefore, to arrange the wedding.

Many guests were invited, and the wedding began. Everyone was happy, and the distinguished guests began to bring forth their costly wedding gifts. When most of the guests had laid into the bowl what they wished, Cabe arose and asked the prince for permission to go out on a necessary errand.

"Oh, I do so want to piss," he whispered to his bridegroom.

"Oh, do be quiet and stay a little," said the prince.

"Ow! Now I want to piss and shit," said Cabe. And with that, he put the finest and most precious of the gifts that had been laid on the table down in his clothes, stood up, and hurried out. The guests were not a little astounded at such peculiar behaviour, but they remained seated, in the hope that the presumed princess would soon come in again. They waited and they waited, but in vain. Then they began to search thoroughly and in every direction, but they did not find the princess. The prince was so sorrowful with grief at this that he went and hanged himself.

This accident, as might be expected, bitterly affected the king. And when he understood the condition that both of his daughters were in, he grew desperate in his grief. He began to believe that Cabe was still alive, and that it must be he who was the origin also of this, his grief and humiliation.

He pondered for a long time what he should do with Cabe. Finally, he came to the conclusion that it did no good to oppose Cabe with evil. He decided therefore to win Cabe over with good, and thus transform him from his worst and most dangerous enemy to his best and most useful friend.

To this end, he proclaimed everywhere that if Cabe would voluntarily come before him, he would not only forgive him all his terrible pranks, but in regard to the great kindness and skill he had shown, he would reward him as honestly and regally as possible. He would, he said, give him one of his daughters and half his kingdom while he himself lived, and the whole kingdom when his days were over. "For," he said, "the one who is wise in one thing is probably also wise in another. And if Cabe understands how to rule my kingdom as well as he has understood to pull my nose, then my daughter can wish for no better husband, and my kingdom for no better king."

Cabe came and received the royal offer. He married the king's eldest daughter, and received at once half the kingdom. When the king a short time later died, he was proclaimed king of the whole realm. The shrewdness that before had distinguished Cabe followed him on to the throne, and caused him to be as loved by his subjects as he was feared by his enemies, whom he was always able to deceive. Cabe reigned always well, and lived a long time. And if he be not dead, then yet he lives. But on which of the world's thrones he rules, of that the story dare not tell.

— 47 —

Scruff

Collector Moltke Moe
Informant Gonil Dalen
Location Bø, Telemark
Year 1878

ONCE UPON A TIME, there was a man who was very stubborn, and he would grant no one houseroom. And there was a vagabond called Scruff, and he said that he would go to this man on Christmas Eve, and be given houseroom.

"Oh, you are insane, you are! You know that he never grants anyone houseroom, and especially not on Christmas Eve," said folk to him.

But Scruff would go anyway. So he took his horse and travelled to the man. He knocked at the door and the maid came out.

"I wanted to ask for houseroom tonight," said Scruff. "Is the man home?"

"It does no good at all," she said; "he never grants anyone houseroom, and certainly not on Christmas Eve."

But he continued to insist, and pretended not to hear what she said. Finally the girl went in again, and the boy came out to try to make Scruff understand that there was no houseroom for him, there on the farm. But Scruff continued to insist. And when it did not help that the wife went out, the man himself went out to Scruff.

"I want to ask for houseroom tonight," said Scruff.

"I don't give houseroom," said the man, "and certainly not on Christmas Eve."

"Oh, many thanks and honour," said Scruff. "Where shall I leave my horse?"

"I don't give houseroom, I say," said the man.

"Oh, many thanks and honour. Yes, it will be good enough to leave him under the barn bridge."

Then he came in, and said thanks and honour for all things. Then they decided that they would cook porridge, and that they should ladle the sour-cream porridge on to one side of the bowl, and pig swill on the other side, where Scruff sat.

As thought, so done.

"Oh, many thanks and honour," said Scruff, as he sat down at the table. "Well, my father was a skipper," he said, "but he did not turn his boat as quickly as I can turn this bowl." And with that, he turned the bowl so that the pig swill came directly before the man, who could not eat a thing.

Then they should go to bed. Scruff should sleep in the sheepfold.

"Oh, many thanks and honour; that is good enough," said Scruff.

When the man had gone in again, he took his horse and placed it in the stable, and the man's horse and left it under the barn bridge. And then he crept into the cabin again; he did not really want to stay in the sheepfold.

And the man was very hungry, so his wife went for some sour cream, some sweet milk, and some wheat flour, and baked a cake for him. Scruff, crouching down, crept in and took the cake. When it was baked, the wife had placed it on the table. In its stead, Scruff shit on the table.

Then the man groaned, and said he was hungry.

"Well, you can take the cake that is on the table," she said.

Well, he was about to eat: "This cake is raw!" he said.

"No, it cannot be raw," said the wife, "as long as I let it bake. But follow me to the pantry, and you shall have something else," she said.

But the man had enough to do with what he was eating that he did not hear his wife. So Scruff crept out after her. And then he had some food; and then they went to bed and looked after one another. Then Scruff crept out.

But then the man groaned and said he was hungry.

His wife said from the cabin said: "I know you cannot be hungry now, so much you have had. And then you lay with me, too," she said.

"Oh, now that Scruff has been there, too!" said the man. He understood how things had gone, for he had seen Scruff in the cabin. With that, he took an axe, went out under the barn bridge, and chopped the head off the horse that stood there.

In the morning, they saw that Scruff had left, and that the man had chopped the head off his own horse. But from then on, the man was kind, and granted houseroom to anyone.

— 48 —

The Three Suitors

Collector Rasmus Leland
Location Rogaland

Once upon a time, there was a girl who was very rich and greedy, and she had crowds of suitors. Once, three came at the same time, all of whom would all bring their suit.

They should stay there for the night, and the girl took them to the bunk house in the evening, and showed them a big bed that all three of them should lie in. But she stole herself up onto the ramp, and would listen to what they spoke about.

As the night drew on, it began to storm and blow outside, and the wind blew up to an awful gale. One of the suitors began to fret, and worry for some great ships that he had out at sea, and lament that they might be lost in the bad weather. The girl then understood that he must be terribly rich, and she thought to herself that she would take *him*.

But then the second suitor began to fret for some great houses that he had built, and lament that they might blow down in the storm. The girl then understood that he had to be at least as rich, so she thought to herself that she would rather have *him*.

The third one said nothing for a long time, and so she thought that he must be a poor unfortunate soul, since he had nothing to lament and fret about. But just as he lay there, he said to one of the others: "Would you move a little, there? You are lying so heavily on the loop of my member," he said.

Then they fell silent, and fell asleep, the three of them.

When they got up in the morning, the girl pretended that she had not heard a thing. And she was pleasant to them all. But she wanted to test them first, before she gave any of them an answer, she said. So she took them out, and told them to run a race around a large field, and he who came first would have her, she said.

So they set off, and ran as quickly as they possibly could, all three. And soon it looked as if he who had nothing to fret and worry about would come in after the other two. And then the girl could not help herself, but began shouting: "You there, with the huge cock! Run straight across! Run straight across, and you will come first!"

He was not slow to do as she had said, and he came first. And that is how he won both the girl, and her riches.

— 49 —

The Boy Who Served the King for Three Years for Three Shillings

Collector H. H. Nordbø
Informant Halvor Nistaas
Location Bø, Telemark
Year 1879/ 80

There was a boy who served the king for three years for three shillings. When the three years were over, the boy got three shillings, and with them he skipped off, as happy as a wagtail in the spring. Soon the boy met an old pauper, who asked him why he was so happy.

"Oh, I have served the king for three years for three shillings," answered the boy.

"If you have as much as three shillings, you can give me one of them," said the pauper.

"I believe I can," said the boy. So the pauper got a shilling.

The boy skipped and ran on his way, and soon he again met an old pauper.

"What is it you are so happy about, then?" asked the pauper.

"Oh, I have served the king for three years for three shillings," said the boy.

"If you have as much as three shillings, you can give me one of them," said the pauper. So the boy gave the pauper the shilling, and skipped off again, just as happy as before. Soon the boy again met an old pauper, who asked what it was he was so happy about.

"Oh, I have served the king for three years, for three shillings," said the boy.

"You can let me have one, and then you can wish for three things," said the pauper.

So the pauper got the shilling, and the boy wished for three things: first God's grace and friendship, then a money pouch that would never be empty, and then he wished that every cunt could speak.

Now that the boy had his money pouch that was never empty, he dressed himself like the most prominent gentleman, and travelled to a princess, to propose. The boy looked so fine and proper, and the princess liked him well enough. At night, the boy and the princess were each to lie in their own chamber, but these chambers were so close that there was but a door between them. During the night, the boy got up and went in to the princess, lifted her eiderdown, and asked if she were a maiden.

"A whore of seven children," she answered (it appears that her cunt spoke here, as the boy had wanted). When the boy heard this, he did not want the princess, but went on his way.

The boy travelled then to a king's daughter, and would propose. That night, he and the king's daughter should each lie in their own chamber, but the chambers were so close that there was but a door between them. During the night, the boy got up out of bed and went in to the king's daughter, lifted her eiderdown, and asked if she were a maiden.

"A whore of five children," she (the cunt) said. When the boy heard this, he would not have her either, but travelled again.

When the princess and the king's daughter understood that the boy had fooled them into talking, they were so angry that they brought him before the Thing. Before the princess went to the Thing, she stuffed some moss in her cunt. When the boy arrived at the Thing, he went straight over to the princess, lifted her skirt, and asked how many children she had had.

"Seven, even though they stuck some moss in me," she (meaning the cunt) said. With that, the matter was decided and the boy was let off.

Then the boy came to some respectable folk, and there was a fine maid there. The boy proposed to the maid, and won her. And they held a feast and lived well and good, for you know, the boy had a money pouch that was never empty.

— 50 —

The Boy and the Parson

Collector Moltke Moe
Informant Gunnar Aarmoti
Location Bø, Telemark
Year 1878

ONCE UPON A TIME, there was a boy who came to a man to ask to go into service. This man had lazy servants; they would do nothing. So he chased them away, and took this boy on instead. And he was so accomplished that it was satisfying.

Now, the wife was fooling around with the parson, and so she had cooked some sour-cream porridge for him, while her husband and the boy were down in the field. But then the boy wanted to go up and see what the woman was so busy with. And she had hidden the parson in a sack of rye sheaves.

When the man also came up, the boy said:

"I do believe the barn roof is sinking."

"Then you should go and take a look," said the man.

So the boy went out to thresh. And he took the sack of rye that the parson lay in, and beat him almost to death. The parson pleaded for himself, and promised him ten barrels of rye, if he did not say anything.

Yes, the man thought this boy was very accomplished, who could thresh so much rye that it was satisfying.

Then they should go to bed. And the boy would lie on the edge, on the outside. "I have such terrible nose bleeds," he said. So the man lay in the middle, and his wife lay closest to the wall.

Then the parson came, and wanted in to the wife. But the boy had his knife ready, and he sliced the parson's cock off, so his blood sprayed across the floor.

The parson hurried home.

The man soon heard that the parson lay ill. And they were such good neighbours, the parson and the man, so he said to his wife:

"You should cook him some sour-cream porridge, and take it to the parson."

So the wife did so. And the boy wanted to go with her.

"It is so heavy, the porridge," he said. "I shall help you."

When they came to the parsonage, the boy said:

"Wait a little; allow me to adjust your clothes." And with that, he hung the parson's cock by a fishing hook, on her clothes. So when the woman came in to the parson, and he saw this, he thought that she had cut off his cock. And he was so angry that he chased her out, with the porridge.

When the woman came home, and took off her clothes, she also saw it. And she was so angry that she chased the boy out.

And that is all there is.

— 51 —

The Soldier Who Went with a Complaint to the King

Collector Moltke Moe
Informant Andres Lia
Location Bø, Telemark
Year 1878

Once upon a time, there was a soldier who would complain to the king about how their company suffered.

"No, you must by no means do that," said the others to him. "You must not go to the king with such, for they are killed who do so."

"That makes no difference," said the soldier; "they see themselves how we fare. There must be an answer."

And with that, off he went. But then he got lost in a great forest, and he wondered around it until he came to a cave of robbers. When they saw this fellow, they began to sharpen their knives, and said that they would make an end of him. Just like that, there came another fellow, who also was lost, and it was the king himself. But he was dressed like any other man, so that they knew him not. Then they grew more eager in their sharpening, for they would have the king, too.

Then the soldier said: "it would be good to make some sport this evening."

Yes, they thought so, too.

"Do you have any pitch?" the soldier asked.

Yes, they had pitch.

"Well, put a cauldron of pitch on," said the soldier, "and I shall make some sport. But I don't suppose you have an iron ladle."

Yes, he got one of those, too.

Then the king would go to watch.

"What the devil do you want?" said the soldier. "Haven't you seen this many times?" And with that, he struck the king beneath his ear so that he retreated to a corner. He did this twice more, and so the king had to stay in his corner.

But the robbers crowded around the soldier, and would see his sport. So he dipped the iron ladle, and cast boiling pitch into their eyes, and thus he killed them, every one. Then there was just him and the king and a girl left, whom the robbers had taken to look after them. Then the soldier went and found a cask of brandy, and then he poured himself a dram, and the king a dram. Then he took the girl, threw her on the bed, and clambered on to her. When he was finished, he wanted the king to do the same, but he would not.

"So pour me a dram, and I will have another turn," he said. And then he chased the girl away. "Now you can go to your home," he said.

And then he burned the whole place up.

Then the king asked him where he was going. Well, he was going to the king with a complaint. He was a soldier, he said. "But where are you from, then?" he asked.

Well, the king mentioned a place, too, but said nothing about being the king. With that, he mounted his horse and rode on ahead, for now, in the light of day, he knew where he was.

Then he said, when he had come home, that they should make up a room for the soldier who would come after. And they should lay forth food for him, but neither spoon nor knife, and then they should tell him he would be killed.

So when the soldier arrived, they said to him: "What do you want here, then?"

"Oh yes, I am a soldier, and I have a complaint for the king."

"Oh you poor thing," they said. "You will be killed; they mostly are who come here with such."

"That cannot be helped," said the soldier. "Right must be right, and that's an end to it." With that, he sat down to eat. But when he found no spoon or knife, he broke off some bread, hollowed it out with his fingers, and slurped his soup with that. This the king had stood watching from behind a pane of glass in the door. Then they said to him: "Now the king has said that you shall die in three days, for you came here with such. So now you are finished."

Then he saw the king in the courtyard, but he did not recognise him, for the king wore his regalia. But when the three days had passed, then the king revealed himself to him, and said that for wages he would have his daughter and half the kingdom. He made his complaint, too.

— 52 —

The Canny Boy

Collector Rasmus Løland
Location Rogaland

ONCE UPON A TIME, there was a boy who should go into service. So he came to a man to negotiate his wages. And he did not demand much. He would work for nothing until the wife of the house began to speak in foreign tongues, he said; but should she do so, then he should have a hundred dollars.

Well, the man quickly agreed to this, for he could never believe that his wife would ever speak in a foreign tongue.

When the boy had been there a short while, he said that he did not like to sleep alone. He was so afraid, he said, that he would have to lie with the farmer folk. The husband was reluctant, but eventually agreed that the boy could sleep at the front of the bed. He should lie in the middle, and his wife against the wall. But the boy was not satisfied with this. It was not fitting that the wife should lie against the wall, he said. She should lie between them, where it was nice and warm, and he would lie against the wall, he said. And he continued to nag until the man agreed to this, too.

Now it happened that the parson in the village had come to the farm on the same evening, and should stay until the morning. He was a great friend of the farmer folk, and often came to spend the night. He slept in a small chamber beside the parlour, and had his bed on the other side of the wall from the bed in the parlour. And that is where he lay this night, too.

When they had gone to bed, and the man and his wife had fallen asleep, the boy heard some scraping from the bed where the parson lay. And just like that, something came probing and poking through a knothole in the wall, just by him. It was the parson, who had stuck his member in like that, and wanted to reach the woman. She usually lay tight against the wall, and they had intercourse with each other in this manner each time the parson was there at night. And now, when the boy saw this, he was not slow. He took his pocket knife and sliced the whole of the parson's member off, and put it in his pocket. Then he lay down to sleep, as if he knew nothing of it.

When they got up in the morning, things fared badly with the parson. He was both pale and poorly to look at. But they could not get out of him what the matter was with him. He was just very sorrowful, and in pain, and he went away.

The woman thought this was unfortunate and painful, so she went off and cooked a great bowl of porridge that she would go to the parson with, and make sure to appease him. The servant boy went with her, to carry the porridge. And when they had gone some way, he took the parson's member out of his pocket and slipped it into the porridge without the woman seeing. The parson was still very sorrowful and in pain, when they arrived. And at first he would neither see them nor receive the porridge. But at length, the woman persuaded him to taste a little of it. But he had not taken many spoonfuls before he found something untoward in the porridge, and he quickly saw what it was, too. Had he been angry before, then he got no better now. And he thought it was the woman who had both used the knife on him and now done this afterwards, to make a complete fool of him. He threw aside the spoon, and ran straight at the woman. But she understood nothing, and thought only that it was passionate play from him, and that he would kiss her. She made herself as happy as a lark, and poked her tongue out at him, and before she knew anything more, he had bitten her tongue right off, and chased her out the door.

When the woman came home, she was both pale and poorly, and could not say a proper word. She just drooled and said, "baba, baba." Her husband first thought she had lost her mind, but when the servant boy came in, he said: "It is easy to hear, this is. She has begun to speak in foreign tongues. And I shall have my pay," he said.

Well, in the end, the man understood that it must be so, him too, and so he had to find the money. Then the boy went on his way, and had a hundred dollars in his pocket for only two-three days' work.

— 53 —

Hans from Tinn

Collector Rikard Berge
Informant Jorund Verpe
Location Bø, Telemark
Year 1914

It was in the time that Norway lay under Denmark that there was disquiet, you know, on account of the king's officials; and so there was sent a terribly good fellow from Tinn, whose name was Hans, to go to Denmark to get some justice and satisfaction on this matter. Down in Denmark, he came upon a great forest, and there he came across a knight who was so stately that it was terrible, with a sword and such. They fell in together, and began to talk, too, until they came to a cabin where there was a light. There they were allowed to stay.

As they sat down at the table, twelve robbers came in, and they ingratiated themselves with them as best they could. But Hans overheard them talking among themselves, that Hans they would have, for he was a big, strong fellow, but the other one they would kill.

There were ten Danes, a Swede, and a Norwegian they called Guttorm Nordman. He was betrothed to Ragnhild, the girl in the house. And then there was an old mother for the robbers—she was there, too.

As the evening drew on, the Swede began to wrestle with Hans, and it turned into a fight between them. But Hans merely defended himself. When it then grew so serious that it became a fight to the death, Hans stabbed him in the heart.

The stranger fellow climbed up on the porch, on some loose planks, and as he crawled forward, to see, then the planks fell down with him on them, straight on to the head of Guttorm Nordman, and knocked him unconscious.

Then the stranger fellow killed three, and Hans killed seven, and that was the end of them.

As they were retiring for the evening, Hans said:

"Well, now we each have a bed, so now you can choose whom you will have, whether you will lie with the old one, or prefer the young one." The stranger fellow did not answer, and so Hans took and threw Ragnhild up into his bed.

"You will want the young one, I suppose," he said. Then he bound his sword to the bed post, and closed it off.

"Now no one gets out," said Hans. And then he lay down with the old woman, and slept straight away. But the old woman wanted to get up, and do something bad, but then she ran straight against the sword, and stabbed herself to death. And so that was the end of her, too.

The next day, Hans went with the stranger fellow; he was going to the king's farm, he said. Hans took one of the robber's horses and rode it. After a little while, they saw the town, and Hans was so jolly and glad.

He met a man, and he said to him:

"If you will kiss my horse's arse, then you can have it," he said.

Well, he did so; he kissed it both behind and before, and so Hans would give him the horse. But then he began to make mischief with the horse, too, did Hans; he jumped over him and did many tricks.

Then they came to some terribly fine houses. This Hans understood to be the king's farm; and everyone bowed before this fellow; and Hans went quiet, too, for then he understood that it was the king he had been together with.

In the evening, he said it:

"Which one would you rather have, the old one or the young one?" said the king. Now, he had a queen, you know, and a daughter. Hans did not answer, but held his tongue. "You will probably want the young one, I think," he said, and then he threw the young one up into Hans's bed. And that is how Hans won the king's daughter; and there was a King Hans.

And then he put things right with the officials at Tinn, too.

— 54 —

The Yule Buck and the Girl

Collector Ole Tobias Olsen
Informant Nils J. Olsen Bjeldaanæs
Location Rana, Nordland
Year 1870

ONE AUTUMN a long time ago, there was such a long drought that the millrace dried up for folk. They had to use a hand mill to grind their flour and malt.

So there was a girl who sat milling for all she was worth, day after day, but it helped little, and she grew less and less eager, and more and more bored of it. Just as she sat like that, the Yule buck came to her and asked if she wanted help with the milling.

"I wouldn't say no to that," replied the girl, "if only there were someone who would."

"I shall help you," said the buck, "if I may lie with you Yuletide night."

"Oh, well—yes, I suppose you may," said the girl, a little lazily, "if only I may escape this blessed grinding."

So the buck began to grind, and the girl just sat at her ease, watching.

So it went all autumn; the buck milled so the flour flew, and all the while he sang:

> Grind, grind now like a fool,
> But fourteen days until Yule.
> As Yuletide night draws on,
> I'll sleep on a maiden's bosom.

But on Yuletide eve, the girl became horrified. She went to the farmer and told him of the wages she had promised the buck for milling, and asked for advice.

"Don't be afraid," said the man. "I shall help you."

So when the evening came, and the girl should go to bed, he took a cauldron of pitch and hung it over the fire until it was at the point of boiling, and then he put it in the bed before her.

A while later something came thundering up the stairs and into the loft, straight towards the bed. There it tore off its clothes, and sat right in the cauldron of pitch. And then there was a dance, perhaps! The buck got up as quickly as he could, and went through the door with a screech and a scream:

> Ow! Ow! The Christian girl was hot!
> She was hot! She was hot!
> She was burning hot!

Sources

The tales in the present volume come from the following sources:

- Asbjørnsen, Moe, Nauthella, et al. *Erotiske folkeeventyr*. Oddbjørg Høgset (ed.). Oslo: Universitetsforlaget, 1977.
- Asbjørnsen, Moe, Nauthella, et al. *Erotiske folkeeventyr*. Oslo: De norske Bokklubbene, 2012.
- Asbjørnsen, Moe, Nauthella, et al. *Erotiske folkeeventyr*. Oslo: Kagge forlag, 2001.
- The online archives of Norsk Folkeminnesamling

About the Translator

My name is Simon Roy Hughes, and I was born in London in 1970. At the age of 21, I ran away to Sweden, then moved to Norway, where (in no particular order) I have earned my education, raised my kids, and settled down. I currently live in Bodø, a city about 100 km north of the Arctic circle.

Despite the impression given by the contents of this volume, I am interested in all kinds of Norwegian folklore, not just the naughty stuff, and I post final drafts of all of my translations to the web, where they are freely available to read.

Take a look: http://norwegianfolktales.blogspot.com

I am also on Twitter: a57998

Printed in Great Britain
by Amazon